"My grandmother approves of you."

Jake's voice was amused. "She longs to be a great-granny."

Annis gave him a puzzled look. "Whatever has that got to do with me?" she asked.

"I told her I was going to marry you." He sounded so casual she could only gape at him and finally gasp, "You what?"

"Told her that I was going to marry you," Jake repeated patiently.

"But I...you...we don't know each other, we're not even friends," she gasped.

"No?" he questioned. "I thought we were. Initially we may not have taken to each other, but having got to know you, I fancy you're just the wife I'm looking for."

Surely no girl had ever had such a cold-blooded proposal? She said roundly, "I've never heard such nonsense! There's only one reason for marrying someone and that's because you love them." She blushed then, because she had that requirement...but Jake apparently did not.

BETTY NEELS

is also the author of these

Harlequin Romances

Many of these books are available at your local bookseller.

For a free catalog listing all titles currently available,
send your name and address to:

HARLEQUIN READER SERVICE
1440 South Priest Drive, Tempe, AZ 85281
Canadian address: Stratford, Ontario N5A 6W2

All Else Confusion

Betty Neels

Harlequin Books

TORONTO • NEW YORK • LOS ANGELES • LONDON
AMSTERDAM • PARIS • SYDNEY • HAMBURG
STOCKHOLM • ATHENS • TOKYO • MILAN

Original hardcover edition published in 1982
by Mills & Boon Limited

ISBN 0-373-02542-4

Harlequin Romance first edition April 1983

Man with the head and woman with the heart:
Man to command and woman to obey;
All else confusion.

Tennyson, *The Princess*

———————•+•———————

CHAPTER ONE

THE Fothergills were out in force; it wasn't often that they were all home together at the same time. Annis was always there, of course, being the eldest and such a help in running the parish and helping her mother around the house, and contrary to would-be sympathisers, perfectly content with her lot. Mary who came next was in her first year at college and Edward, at seventeen, was in his last term at the public school whose fees had been the cause of much sacrifice on his parents part. James was at the grammar school in a neighbouring town and Emma and Audrey were still at the local church school. So they didn't see much of each other, because holidays weren't always exactly the same and they all possessed so many friends that one or other of them was mostly away visiting one or other of them. But just for once the half term holiday had fallen on the same days for all of them, and since the February afternoon was masquerading as spring, they had all elected to go for a walk together.

Annis led the way, a tall, well built girl with glorious red hair and a lovely face. She looked a good deal younger than her twenty-two years and although she was moderately clever, she had an endearing dreaminess, a generous nature and a complete lack of sophistication. She also, on occasion, made no bones about speaking her mind if her feelings had been strongly stirred.

Mary, walking with Audrey a few paces behind her, was slighter and smaller in build and just as pretty in a dark way, while little Audrey, still plump and youthfully awkward, had her elder sister's red hair and cornflower blue eyes.

Emma and James were together, quarrelling cheerfully about something or other, and Edward brought up the rear, a dark, serious boy who intended to follow in his father's footsteps.

The church and the Rectory lay at one end of Millbury, the village to which their father had brought his young wife and where they still lived in the early Victorian house which had been considered suitable for the rector in those days, and was still suitable for the Reverend Mr Fothergill, considering the size of his family. Certainly it had a great many rooms, some of them far too large and lofty for comfort, but there was only one bathroom with an old-fashioned bath on clawed feet in its centre, and the hot water system needed a good deal of forbearance, while the kitchen, although cosy and plentifully supplied with cupboards, lacked the amenities considered by most people to be quite necessary nowadays. Mrs Fothergill, a gently placid woman, didn't complain, for the simple reason that it would have been of no use; with six children to bring up, clothe and feed, there had never been enough money to spare on the house. Her one consolation was that since she had married young, there was the strong possibility that all the children would be nicely settled in time for her to turn her attention to refurbishing it.

Reaching the top of the hill behind the village, Annis turned to look down at her home. From a distance its red brick walls, surrounded by the shrubbery no one had the time to do much about, looked pleasant in the watery sunshine, and beyond it the church's squat tower stood out against the Wiltshire downs stretching away to more wooded country.

She turned her fine eyes on to her brothers and sisters gathered around her. 'There's plenty of wood in the park,' she suggested, 'Matthew told me that they'd cut down several elms along the back drive. Let's get as much as we can – a pity we didn't bring some sacks, but I forgot.'

'Well, with six of us carrying a load each, we ought to manage quite a lot,' offered James. 'I could go back for some sacks, Annis . . .?'

She shook her head. 'It'll be getting dark in another hour or so—it's not worth it.'

They followed the path running along the edge of the field at the top of the hill and climbed a gate at the end into a narrow lane, and it was another five minutes' walk before they reached the entrance to the back drive to Mellbury Park where Colonel Avery lived. The lodge beside the open gate had fallen into a near ruin and the drive had degenerated into a deeply rutted track, but they all knew their way around and with Annis still leading, started to walk along it. They came upon the cut down trees within a very short time, and just as Annis had said, there was an abundance of wood.

They worked methodically; almost everyone went wooding in the village, and the Fothergills had become experts at knowing what best to take and what best to leave and just how much they could carry. Presently, suitably burdened according to size, they turned for home. The bright afternoon was yielding to a grey dusk; by the time they reached it it would be almost dark. Annis marshalled her little band into a single line with Edward leading the way and herself bringing up the rear. Little Audrey, who was frightened of the dark, was directly in front of her, carrying the few light bits of wood considered sufficient for her strength.

They made a good deal of noise as they went, calling to each other, singing a bit from time to time, laughing a lot. They were almost at the lodge when Annis heard the thud of hooves behind her and stopped to turn the way they had come and shout at the top of her powerful lungs:

'Slow down, Matthew, we're just ahead of you!' And as a young man on a big black horse pulled up within yards: 'Honestly, Matt, you must be out of your mind! You could have bowled the lot of us over like ninepins!'

'No chance of that with you bawling your head off like that—you're in our park anyway!'

'So what? We come here almost every day.' She smiled dazzlingly at him. 'You use our barn for target practice.'

He laughed then, a pleasant-faced young man of about her own age, and shouted greetings to the rest of the Fothergills, scattered along the path ahead of her, then called over his shoulder, 'Jake, come and meet our neighbours!'

The second rider had been waiting quietly, screened by the overgrowth, and Annis hadn't seen him. He was astride a strawberry roan, a big man with powerful shoulders and a handsome arrogant face; it was dusk now and she couldn't be sure of the colour of his eyes or his hair, but of one thing she was instantly sure—she didn't like him, and she didn't like the smile on his face as Matthew introduced him, nor the unhurried study of her person and the still more leisurely survey of the rest of the Fothergills who, seeing that Matthew had someone with him, had come closer to see who it was. Jake Royle, Matthew had called him, a friend of the family who had been in New Zealand on business. 'You must come up and have a drink one evening,' said Matthew, and sidled his horse over to Mary. 'You too, Mary—and Edward, of course.'

'Well, it'll have to be soon,' said Annis briskly. 'Mary is going back at the end of the week, and so is Edward.'

'And you?' queried Jake Royle softly.

She gave him a quick glance. 'Me? I live at home.' He didn't answer, only smiled again, and her dislike deepened. How had Matt got to know him? she wondered; he was much older for a start, at least in his early thirties, and as unlike Matt's usual friends as chalk from cheese. She caught Edward's eye. 'We'd better be on our way; tea's early—it's the Mothers' Union whist drive this evening.'

'Good lord, you don't all play whist, do you?'

'Is there any reason why we shouldn't? Don't be an ass, Matt, you know quite well that only Edward and Mary and I go.' Annis turned to go and then stopped. 'Could you come over when you've got a minute and take a look at Nancy?'

'Yes, of course—we'll come now . . .'

She said hastily: 'Oh, there's no need for that—besides, you have Mr Royle with you. Tomorrow morning would be better.'

'Well, all right, if you say so.'

She said rather pointedly: 'I'll expect you about ten o'clock if that's O.K. for you?' She gave him a wide smile, nodded distantly to Jake Royle, and hurried to join the others, already on their way.

'Lifelong friends?' queried Jake Royle as the Fothergills disappeared round a bend in the track.

'Grew up with them,' said Matthew. 'Annis and I are the same age; knew each other in our prams.'

'A striking-looking girl,' observed Mr Royle, 'and interesting . . .'

An opinion not shared by Annis; on the way back they all discussed Matt's companion. 'He's very good-looking,' said Mary, 'didn't you think so, Annis?'

Annis had been brought up to be honest. 'Yes, if you like that kind of face,' she conceded, 'but I daresay he's the dullest creature, and conceited too.' She added rather unnecessarily: 'I didn't like him.'

'Do you suppose he's married?' asked Emma.

Annis gave the question her considered thought. 'Very likely, I should think. He's not a young man, not like Matt. Whose turn is it to see to Nancy?'

Nancy was an elderly donkey, rescued some years ago from a party of tinkers who were ill-using her. No one knew quite how old she was, but now she lived in retirement, a well fed, well cared for and dearly loved friend to all the family. It was Audrey's turn, and by common consent James went with her to the small paddock behind the house; she was only eight after all, and a small nervous child, and although no one mentioned this fact, her brothers and sisters took good care of her. The rest of them went into the house through the back door, kicking off boots and hanging up coats in the roomy lobby which gave on to the wide stone-flagged passage which ran from front to back of the Rectory. They piled the wood here too, ready for James or Edward to carry out to one of the numerous outbuildings which bordered the yard behind the house. They went next to a cold cupboard of a room used once, long ago, as a pantry, washed their hands at the old stone sink there and tidied their hair at the Woolworth's looking-glass on the wall, only then did they troop along to the front of the house to the sitting room.

Their parents were already there, their father sitting by the fire, his nose buried in a book, their mother at the round table under the window where tea had been laid out. She was still a pretty woman who had never lost her sense of humour or her optimistic belief that one day something wonderful would happen, by which she meant having enough money to do all the things she wanted to do for them all. She looked up as they went in and smiled at them impartially; she loved them all equally, although perhaps little Audrey had the edge of her brothers and sisters, but then she was still only a little girl.

She addressed herself to her eldest child: 'You enjoyed your walk, Annis?'

'Yes, Mother.'

Before she could say anything more Mary chimed in: 'We met Matt—he had someone with him, Jake Royle, he's staying with the Avery's. He's quite old but rather super . . .'

'Old?' queried her mother.

'About thirty-five,' observed Annis, slicing cake. 'I thought he looked a bit cocky, myself.'

Her father lowered his book. 'And he has every reason to be,' he told her with mild reproof. 'He's a very clever young man—well, I consider him young—he's chairman of several highly successful companies and commercial undertakings, owns a factory in New Zealand, and is much sought after as a financial adviser.'

Annis carried tea to her father. 'Do you know him, Father?'

'Oh, yes, I've met him on several occasions at Colonel Avery's.'

'You never told us,' said Mary.

'You said yourself that he was quite old, my dear.' His voice was dry. 'Far too old for you—perhaps he and Annis might have more in common.'

'Me?' Annis paused with her cup half way to her mouth. 'I don't know a thing about factories or finances—besides, I didn't like him.'

'Well, we're not likely to see him here, dear,' said Mrs Fothergill calmly, hoping that they would. 'Here's Audrey and James, perhaps you'd fill the teapot, dear . . .'

It was later that evening, after the younger ones had gone to bed and the rest of them were sitting round the comfortably shabby room, that Mrs Fothergill said apropos nothing at all: 'I wonder if Mr Royle is married?'

Neither Edward or James was interested enough to answer and Mary had gone to the kitchen for something. Annis said thoughtfully: 'I should think so; you say he's successful and clever and probably comfortably off. Besides, he's getting on for forty . . .'

'You said thirty-five, dear,' observed her mother. 'I should imagine that a man who has achieved so

much has had little time to look for a suitable wife.'
She didn't say any more, and Annis, glancing up
from her embroidery, saw that her mother was day-
dreaming—marrying off her daughters, or one
daughter at least to Jake Royle. He would have
given her loads of money, a huge house, several cars
and a generous nature not above helping out with
the younger children's education. Well, harmless
enough, thought Annis fondly, just as long as Mary
was to be the bride. Mr Royle, married or un-
married, held no attraction for her at all.

So it was a pity that he rode over with Matt the
next morning, blandly ignoring her cold reception,
contriving with all the ease in the world to get introduced to her mother, and her father as well, before
going off with Matt to look at Nancy. What was
more, she was quite unable to refuse Matt's cheerful:
'Come on, old girl—if it's Nancy's hooves we'll need
your help.'

So the three of them crossed the cobbled yard to
where Nancy lived in a boxed-off corner of the enormous barn. Once the days were longer and it was
warmer she would go out in the small field behind
this building, sharing it with a neighbouring farmer's
two horses and a couple of goats, but today she was
standing in her snug shelter very neat and tidy after
little Audrey's grooming.

She knew Matt as well as her owners and obediently lifted first one hoof and then the other, munching the carrots Annis had thoughtfully brought
with her and responding, much to Annis's surprise,
with every sign of pleasure to Jake Royle's gentle
scratching of her ears.

'Must like you,' observed Matt, looking up. 'She's

a crotchety old lady with strangers. Still got some
serviceable teeth, too.'

'Yes, you said she was off her feed.' He slid a large,
well manicured hand from an ear to the little beast's
lip and lifted it gently. 'Could there be an abscess, I
wonder?' He uttered the question in such a friendly,
almost meek voice, that Annis, prepared to snub him
at every turn, found herself saying: 'I hadn't thought
of that—she's always having trouble with her feet
and I expected it to be that this time.' She tickled
Nancy's other ear. 'Open your mouth, love.'

It took the remaining carrots and the three of
them to persuade Nancy to allow them to take a
look at her teeth. Annis, with her fiery head almost
in Nancy's jaws and quite forgetting that she didn't
like Jake Royle, exclaimed: 'You're quite right, how
clever of you! It's at the back on the right.' She
withdrew her hand. 'I'll get the vet.'

Matt said: 'Oh, hard luck—he's just put up his
fees, too.'

'I've got some birthday money left,' said Annis
matter-of-factly. She had forgotten that Jake Royle
was still there; he had a stillness which made him
invisible, a knack of melting into his surroundings.
He didn't move now, only stared hard at her. She
made a striking picture too, despite the old coat and
wellingtons, and her hair in a wavy tangled mass.
She tossed it impatiently out of her eyes and invited
them into the Rectory for coffee. 'You'll have to have
it in the kitchen,' she warned them, 'we're getting
the sitting room ready for the Mothers' Union tea-
party.'

She gave Nancy a final pat and led them back
and through the kitchen door where they kicked off

their boots and laid them neatly beside hers. Even in his socks Jake Royle was a very large man indeed.

The kitchen was large, stone-flagged and old-fashioned. There were no built-in cupboards, concealed ironing boards bread bins or vegetable racks and the sink was an enormous one of well scrubbed Victorian stone. But it was a pleasant room, much used by the whole family, its plain wooden table encircled by an assortment of chairs and two down-at-heel armchairs on either side of the elderly Aga, put in by the rector the winter before last in an effort to modernise the place. Both chairs were occupied, a seal point Siamese was sitting erect in one of them, the other was occupied by a rather tatty dog with quantities of long hair and a sweeping tail. Neither of them took any notice of the newcomers although Matt said: 'Hullo, Sapphro, hullo Hairy,' as he took his seat at the table.

'Sit down, Jake,' said Mrs Fothergill invitingly. 'You don't mind if I call you that?—Mr Royle's so stiff, isn't it? Coffee's just ready—everyone will be here in a minute.'

Annis had gone to phone the vet and came back with little Audrey, the rest of them following. Only the Rector didn't arrive. 'His sermon,' explained Mrs Fothergill. 'He likes to beat it into shape before lunch.'

She poured coffee into an assortment of mugs and Annis bore one away for her father. She would have liked to have taken hers too, but that might have looked rude and her mother was a great one for manners—besides, being the eldest she had to set a good example to the others.

Over coffee, Jake Royle maintained an easy flow

of talk without pushing himself forward; he merely
introduced topics of conversation from time to time
and then left it to everyone else to talk. And the
Fothergills were great talkers; being such a large
family they held different opinions about almost
everything—besides, it was a way of passing the
evenings. There wasn't much to do in the village and
Millbury was off the main road which ran between
Shaftesbury and Yeovil; too far to walk to the bus,
although Annis did a good deal of cycling round the
village and the two smaller parishes her father
served. There was a car, of course, an essential for
her father with such a far-flung flock, but it had seen
better days and it was heavy on petrol too. Only the
Rector, Annis and Edward drove it, nursing it along
the narrow lanes and up and down the steep hills.
Mrs Fothergill, a born optimist, went in for every
competition which offered a car as prize, but as yet
she had had no luck. One day the car was going to
conk out and would have to be replaced, but no one
dwelt on that. When tackled the Rector was apt to
intone 'Sufficient unto the day . . .' which put a stop
to further speculation.

They were talking about cars now, at least the men
and three boys were. Anyone would think, thought
Annis gloomily, that there was nothing else upon
this earth but cars. She listened to the more interesting bits, but in between she allowed her mind to
wander. She still didn't like Jake Royle, but she had
to admit that he had more than his share of good
looks, and the very size of him made him someone to
look at twice. Not that she had the least interest in
him . . . She picked up the big enamel coffee pot
from its place on the Aga and offered second cups,

caught his eye and blushed because it was only too apparent that he had read her thoughts.

He and Matt went presently and Mrs Fothergill said a little wistfully: 'What a very nice man. I suppose he'll be going back to New Zealand soon—such a pity.'

'He doesn't live there,' Edward observed, 'only goes there once in a while—he had intended going back in a couple of weeks, but he said that something had come up to make him change his mind.'

Mrs Fothergill couldn't help taking a quick peep at her two elder daughters. Mary looked pleased and surprised, Annis's lovely face wore no expression upon it at all. Nor did she show any elation when later that day Mrs Avery telephoned to ask them, with the exception of James, Emma and little Audrey, to go to dinner in two days' time. Mrs Fothergill and Mary immediately fell to discussing what they should wear, but when they tried to draw Annis into the discussion, she proved singularly uninterested.

'It'll have to be the blue velvet,' she told them. 'I know I've had it years, but this isn't London and fashion hasn't changed all that much.'

A statement with which Mr Royle couldn't agree. He dated it unerringly as being five years old and on the dowdy side, bought with an eye to its being useful rather than becoming. But the dark blue set off the hair very well, he conceded that, and the dress, however badly cut, couldn't disguise her splendid figure. She was a young woman who would look magnificent if she were properly dressed.

He greeted her with casual politeness and engaged her mother in conversation, while Matt made his way across the drawing-room to ask her how Nancy did. They became engrossed in the donkey's treatment and exactly what had been done, but presently they were joined by Mrs Avery, and with a hurried promise to come over on the following morning, Matt wandered off to talk to Mary.

The dinner party was small, the Fothergills being augmented by the doctor and his wife and daughter, and since they had all lived in the village for years, they were on the best of terms. Presently they all went across the gloomy raftered hall to the dining room, an equally gloomy room, its walls oak-panelled and the great table ringed by antique and uncomfortable chairs. Colonel Avery never ceased grumbling about them, but since the idea of replacing family heirlooms with something more modern wasn't to be entertained, everyone put up with them in silence.

But even though the room was gloomy, the people in it weren't: the talk became quite animated as they ate their way through chilled melon, roast beef, Yorkshire pudding, roast potatoes and sprouts and rounded off this very English meal with Charlotte Russe. There was Stilton after that, and since Mrs Avery was too old-fashioned to change her ways, the ladies, very animated after the excellent claret the Colonel had given them, left the men round the table and went back to the drawing-room.

Here Mrs Avery, a mouselike woman whose appearance belied her forceful personality, set about arranging her guests to her satisfaction. The doctor's wife and Mrs Fothergill were seated side by side on one of the sofas, Mary and the doctor's daughter were marshalled on to a smaller piece of furniture and Mrs Avery herself engaged Annis in conversation, sitting so that she could see the door when the men came in. For years now she had decided that Annis would make a very good wife for Matt. They had grown up together and liked each other, and Annis would do very nicely as mistress of the Manor House in which the Avery family had lived for a very long time. She lost no time, once she had decided upon this, in throwing them together on every possible occasion. It was a pity that neither Annis nor Matt had any inkling of this, and continued to see each other several times a week without feeling any desire to be more than good friends.

The men joined them quite soon and Mrs Avery signalled with her eyebrows to Matt that he should join them, only to be frustrated by Jake Royle, who somehow contrived to get there first and stayed inextricably with them until she was forced to circulate amongst her other guests.

Which left Annis on the sofa, rather apart from the others, and Jake Royle sitting beside her, half turned towards her so that he could watch her face.

'Was the vet able to do anything for Nancy?' he enquired in such a friendly voice that she found herself replying readily enough. They discussed the donkey at some length, and then, almost imperceptibly, he led the conversation round to her family and eventually to herself. He had discovered quite a lot about her before she realised what was happening and closed her pretty mouth with a suddenness which made him chuckle silently. She shot him a look as fiery as her hair and asked with something of a snap: 'And when do you return to New Zealand, Mr Royle?'

'I'm called Jake,' he reminded her gently, 'and I don't really know when I shall go there again. I live in England, you know.'

'No, I didn't. Do you like New Zealand?'

'Very much. Have you travelled at all, Annis?'

She had to admit that beyond a week in Brittany some years previously, and a long weekend in Brussels with a school friend, she hadn't.

'You would like to travel?' he persisted.

'Well, of course. I should think everyone would, some places more than others, of course.'

'And those places?'

She knitted her strong brows. There was no end to the tiresome man's questions, and why couldn't someone come and take him away? 'Oh, Canada and Norway and Sweden and Malta and the Greek Isles and Madeira.'

He said lightly: 'Let's hope you have the opportunity to visit some or all of them at some time or another.'

'Yes—well, I hope so too. And now, if you'll excuse me, I really must have a word with Colonel Avery about . . .' She had no idea what; he helped her out with a casual 'Yes, of course—time passes so quickly when one is enjoying a pleasant talk.'

She got up and he got up too, and she edged away, relieved to see that Miriam, Doctor Bennett's daughter, was poised to take her place. From the safety of the other end of the room, she saw the pair of them obviously enjoying each other's company. The sight quite annoyed her.

Half-term finished the next day and Annis was alone once more then with her mother and father and old Mrs Wells who did for them twice a week.

She had come to the Rectory, year in, year out, for a long time and her work—doing the rough, she called it—had by tacit consent been honed down to jobs like polishing the brass, sitting comfortably at the kitchen table, or peeling the potatoes for lunch. But no one thought of telling her that she might retire if she wanted to. For one thing she didn't want to; she lived alone in the village and the Rectory supplied an interest in her life; besides, she would have been missed by all the family, who cheerfully cleared up after her, found her specs, gave her cups of tea and took the eyes out of the potatoes when she wasn't looking. She was devoted to all of them and went regularly to church, besides attending all the jumble sales, where she purchased her wardrobe, dirt cheap, three times a year.

She sat at the kitchen table now, mending a great rent in the sheet James had put his feet through, while Annis juggled with the washing machine. It was behaving temperamentally this morning, making a terrible din, oozing water from somewhere underneath, and having long bouts of doing nothing at all. Mrs Fothergill, coming into the kitchen to make the coffee, gave it a harassed look. 'Is it going to break down?' she shouted to Annis above the din.

'Shouldn't think so. I'll give it a rest before I put the next load in.'

Mrs Fothergill nodded. 'Yes, dear. Coffee will be ready in five minutes. We're in the drawing room.'

They almost never used the drawing room; it was a handsome apartment, so large and lofty that it was impossible to keep it really warm. Annis supposed her mother was turning out the sitting room. She made Mrs Wells the pot of strong tea she always fancied mid-morning, emptied the washing machine and went along to the drawing room.

She opened the door and went in, and only then realised that there were visitors—Matt, who didn't really count, Mr Royle and a small, elderly lady, almost completely round as to figure and with a pair of black eyes sparkling in a round face.

Matt and Jake Royle got up and Matt said cheerfully: 'Hullo, Annis. You look as though you're doing a hard day's work. We've brought one of my aunts over—it was Jake's idea. She arrived quite late yesterday evening and went to bed, too tired for the dinner party. Aunt Dora, this is Annis—a pity you've missed the others.'

Annis put a hand up to her hair, realised that it was in a hopeless mess anyway, and offered the hand instead to Matt's aunt.

'You could have told me,' she complained mildly to Matt. She smiled at the little lady. 'I would have tidied myself up.'

'You'll do very well as you are. Matt didn't tell you my name. It's Duvant—I'm the Colonel's sister and a widow.' She accepted a cup of coffee from Mrs Fothergill and patted the sagging sofa she was sitting on. 'Come and sit by me. Your mother's an angel to receive us so kindly, too. You must wish us all to kingdom come, but men never think about getting the housework done or cooking lunch, do they? And somehow I had the impression from Jake that you roamed out of doors a good deal . . .'

Annis gave Jake a look of dislike, which became thunderous when he smiled at her. How like him; never done a hand's turn in his life probably, and had no idea what it was like to run an unwieldy old house like the Rectory. She said politely: 'I like being out of doors. Do you know this part of the country well, Mrs Duvant?'

'I did in my youth, but things have changed even here. I've been living abroad for some years, but I fancied coming back here again. There is a house in Bath, which belonged to my husband's family. I think I shall go there for a while.' She paused to smile at Annis. 'This coffee's delicious—I think I'll have another cup if I may?' She beamed across at Mrs Fothergill. 'I expect you grind your own beans?' she asked.

The two ladies embarked on an animated discussion and Jake, refusing more coffee, suggested that they might take a look at Nancy. And since Matt agreed at once there was nothing for it but for Annis to get her coat and boots and go with them. 'Though I can't really spare the time,' she told them rather crossly.

'We'll hang out the washing for you,' offered Jake.

'Thank you,' said Annis haughtily, 'but I can manage very well for myself.'

They spent a little time with Nancy, pronounced her very much better and started back across the yard. At the back door Annis paused. 'I expect you'll want to join Mrs Duvant—I'm going back to the kitchen.'

They neither of them took any notice of her but went along to the kitchen too, collected the old-fashioned basket loaded with damp sheets and towels and bore it off to the washing line at the back of the house. It hadn't been any use protesting; Matt had told her not to be so bossy and Jake Royle had merely smiled. She hadn't liked the smile much, there had been a hint of mockery about it.

She put another load into the machine, tidied herself perfunctorily and went back to the drawing room. Her father had gone, but the two ladies were having a nice gossip; from the way they both turned to look at her and their sudden silence, she suspected that they had been talking about her. Not that that worried her.

Mrs Duvant spoke first. 'I was just telling your mother that I want to go over to Bath and look round that house. She tells me that you drive; I wondered if you would take me one day soon, Annis? Matt says he can't be spared from the estate; they're doing the yearly inventory or some such thing, and Jake will be going to London tomorrow. We could have the Rover.'

Annis glanced at her mother and found that lady looking pleased. 'A nice change for you, darling,' said Mrs Fothergill. 'Just for a couple of days, and there's almost nothing to do now the others are away.'

'Well, yes—then I'd be glad to drive you,' said Annis. It was true she could be spared easily enough, and she liked Mrs Duvant.

The men came in then and Mrs Duvant told them, and Matt said: 'Oh, good, that's settled then,' while Jake Royle said nothing at all. It seemed to be a habit of his.

CHAPTER TWO

THE trip to Bath was planned for two days ahead, midweek, so that Annis would be back for the week-end to drive her father round the three parishes on Sunday and keep an eye on Emma, Audrey and James.

It was a pity that she hadn't anything really smart to wear, she decided as she packed an over-night bag; she could wear her tweed suit, a good one although no longer new, and there was a blouse she had had for Christmas which would do, as well as a sweater, and just in case Mrs Duvant changed in the evening, she could take the green wool jersey dress and wear her gold chain with it. She reflected uneasily upon Mrs Duvant's undoubtedly expensive clothes. She might be a dumpy little woman, but she had been wearing a beautifully cut outfit and doubtless the rest of her wardrobe was as elegant.

Matt drove the Rover, with his aunt in it, over to the Rectory soon after breakfast, declaring that he would walk back through the park. He added a careless: 'Jake went yesterday, gone to keep an eye on his millions—wish I had half his brains. Father's quite peevish this morning; no one to discuss the *Financial Times* with. I bet Jake enjoys himself in town!'

His aunt smiled at him. 'And why not? I should think he could have any girl he wanted with that

27

handsome face of his. Are we ready to go, Annis my dear? I'm quite looking forward to this next day or two. I hope you are too.'

They drove via Frome and Radstock and Midsummer Norton, through a soft grey morning with a hint of frost in the air, and Bath, as they approached it, looked delightful, its grey stone houses clinging to the hills. Annis made her way through the town and then at Mrs Duvant's direction turned into a crescent of Regency houses facing a small park. Half way down she was told to stop and pulled up before a narrow tall house with elegant bow windows just like all its neighbours. She had expected to find an unlived-in house, but this one was freshly painted and bore all the signs of careful tenancy. As she opened the car door she saw the house door open and an elderly man cross the pavement to them.

'Ah, there's Bates,' declared Mrs Duvant happily. 'He and Mrs Bates caretake for me, you know.' She got out of the car and went to shake him by the hand. 'And this is Miss Annis Fothergill,' she told him, 'come to spend a day or two while I look round the place. I've a mind to come back here and live, Bates.'

The elderly man looked pleased. 'And I'm sure we hope that you do, madam. If you will go in, Mrs Bates will see to you. I'll bring the cases.'

The door was narrow with a handsome fanlight above it, and opened into a roomy hall with a pretty curved staircase at its back. Annis had time to see that before Mrs Bates bore down upon them; a large, stately woman with twinkling eyes and several chins.

She received Mrs Duvant with every sign of delight, made Annis welcome, and ushered them into a small sitting-room, most comfortably furnished and with a bright fire blazing in the hearth.

'You'll like a cup of coffee, madam,' she said comfortably. 'When you've had a rest I'll take you up to your rooms.'

She sailed away and Mrs Duvant observed: 'Such a good creature, and a splendid cook.' She looked around her. 'Everything looks very nice after all this time. I'd quite forgotten . . .'

The coffee came and presently Mrs Bates to lead them upstairs and show first Mrs Duvant to a room at the front of the house and then Annis to hers; a charming apartment overlooking the surprisingly large garden at the back. Annis, used to the rather spartan simplicity at the Rectory, poked her head into the adjoining bathroom, smoothed the silken quilt and opened a drawer or two, lined with tissue paper and smelling of lavender. There was a built-in wardrobe too and a couple of small inviting easy chairs. Definitely a room to enjoy, she decided as she tidied herself at the little walnut dressing table, brushed her hair into a glossy curtain, and went downstairs.

Mrs Duvant was in the hall, talking to Bates. 'There's an hour or more before lunch, let's go over the house.' She was as excited as a small child with a new toy.

So with Mrs Bates sailing ahead of them, and Mrs Duvant trotting behind with Annis beside her, they set off. It was to be no lightning tour—that was obvious from the start. Mrs Duvant stopped every few steps to examine curtains, stooped to inspect carpets and insinuate her round person into cupboards. They started with the dining room, an elegantly furnished room with an oval mahogany table and six charming Adam chairs around it; there were half a dozen more chairs against the walls and a handsome sideboard, on which was displayed a selection of silver gilt. The walls were hung with sea green brocade and almost covered with what Annis took to be family portraits. A delightful room; she could find no fault with it, nor for that matter could its owner.

The drawing-room took a good deal longer; it was a large room with white panelling and a China blue ceiling, ornamented with a good deal of plasterwork, and the furniture was plentiful and elaborate; moreover there were innumerable ornaments scattered about its small tables. Annis found it a little too grand for her taste and uttered a sigh of pleasure at the morning room on the other side of the hall, a simple little room which Mrs Duvant dismissed quickly enough. The sitting room they had already seen and by then it was time for lunch, anyway.

Refreshed by oyster soup, omelette with a side salad and a rich creamy dessert, taken with a glass of white wine, Mrs Duvant declared herself ready to inspect the upper floors. And that took most of the afternoon, what with a long discussion about new curtains for one of the bedrooms, and a meticulous inspection of the linen closet on the top floor, but presently they were sitting by the fire having tea and with the prospect of the evening before them.

'I've got tickets for the concert in the Assembly

Rooms, dear,' observed Mrs Duvant. If we have dinner a little early, we shall be in good time for it. It doesn't start before half past eight.'

Going to bed much later, Annis decided that there was a lot to be said for such a pleasant way of life—not that she would want to change it for her life at the Rectory, but like any other girl, she sometimes hankered after the fleshpots.

They spent almost all the next day shopping: Mrs Duvant, it seemed, was a great shopper and since money didn't seem to be any problem to her, she bought several things at prices which made Annis lift her eyebrows, but her companion's enjoyment was so genuine that she could find no objection, and after all, it was her money, and besides, Annis liked her.

They went to a cinema that evening and the following morning drove back with a firm promise to Bates that Mrs Duvant intended to take up residence in the near future.

They reached the Rectory at teatime and while Annis rang Matt to come over and collect the Rover and his aunt, Mrs Fothergill sat Mrs Duvant down before the fire and plied her with tea and hot buttered toast.

It was when Annis joined them that Mrs Duvant, between bites, announced that she would like Annis to accompany her to Bath. 'Just for a few weeks,' she said persuasively. 'I shall be a little lonely at first—if you could spare her? And if she would like to come?' She glanced a little anxiously at Annis. 'It would be a job, of course, I forget things and leave things lying around, and paying bills and so on, so you'd be quite busy, dear. Would forty pounds a week suit you? For about six weeks?'

Two hundred and forty pounds; Mrs Duvant had paid exactly that for a suit in Jaegar's the day before. A list, expanding every second in Annis's head, of things which that sum would buy for them all, slowly unrolled itself before Annis's inward eyes. A washing machine, a new coat for her mother, shoes for the boys, all the tobacco her father could smoke, the dancing slippers little Audrey had set her heart upon . . . She glanced at her mother and saw that she was doing exactly the same thing. She said promptly: 'Well, if Mother could manage, I'd love to come, if you think I'd be of any use.'

'Of course you will. That's settled, then. You've no idea how grateful I am, Annis.' She paused as the door opened and Matt came in. It wasn't until the hubbub of small talk had died down that she said: 'Shall we say on Saturday? That gives you four days. Is that time enough?'

Annis nodded. 'Plenty. Do I drive you again?'

'Yes, I think so. I can have the Rover for the time being. We must see about getting a car later on.' She bustled out on a tide of goodbyes, explaining to Matt as they went.

When the last sounds of the car had died away Mrs Fothergill said: 'You do want to go, darling? I shall miss you, and so will your father, but it will make a nice change and you'll have some money.'

'We'll have some money,' Annis corrected her. 'I've already made a list, have you?'

Her mother nodded happily. 'But it's your money, Annis. Now tell me, what sort of a house is it?'

Annis began to tell her, and it took quite a time; she hadn't quite finished when her father came in from a parish council meeting, and she went to get the supper and make sure that the younger ones were doing their homework properly.

Back at the Manor House, Mrs Duvant was writing a letter. She wrote as she did most things, with enthusiasm and a great many flourishes of the pen and she smiled a good deal as she wrote. It was a long letter. She read it through, put it in an envelope and addressed it to Jake Royle, whose godmother she was.

The house at Bath looked very welcoming as Annis drew up before it on Saturday afternoon. It had been a bright, cold day and now that the sun was almost gone there was a already a sparkle of frost, but the house blazed with lights, and as they went in Annis noticed the great bowl of daffodils on the hall table and in the little sitting room where they at once went, the window held hyacinths of every colour. There was a vase of roses too, long-stemmed and perfect. Mrs Duvant picked up the card with them and chuckled as she read it, although she didn't say why.

'We'd like tea, Bates,' she said briskly, 'I know it's rather late, but perhaps Mrs Bates could put dinner back half an hour?'

So the two of them had tea together round the fire before going upstairs to unpack and get ready for dinner. 'I always like to change my dress,' observed Mrs Duvant. 'Nothing fancy, you know, unless I'm going out, but it somehow makes the evening more of an occasion, if you see what I mean?'

So Annis took the hint and put on the green jersey, wondering as she did so if she might get herself another dress when she was paid. She and her mother had pored over their lists, scratching out and adding until they had spent her wages, on paper at least, to the greatest advantage. Even after everyone had had something there was a little over for herself—enough for a dress—something plain and dateless to take the place of the outworn blue velvet. Doubtless she would have some time to herself in which to browse among the shops. Annis tugged her green jersey into shape with an impatient hand and went downstairs.

She discovered after the first few days that her duties were light in the extreme and consisted mainly in finding Mrs Duvant's spectacles, handbag, library book and knitting whenever she mislaid them, which was often, reminding her of the various things she wished to do each day, and unpicking her knitting when she got it in a muddle; that was pretty often too. The pair of them got on excellently together and since Annis got on equally well with the Bates', the household was a happy one.

She had been there a week when the even tenor of her days was unexpectedly shaken. Mrs Duvant had the habit of retiring for an afternoon nap after lunch each day, leaving Annis to do as she wished. Previously she had gone for a brisk walk, done some window shopping and taken herself round the Roman Baths, but this afternoon it was raining, not a soft rain to be ignored, but a steady, icy downpour. Annis decided on a book by the fire as she came downstairs after seeing Mrs Duvant safely tucked up. There were plenty of books in the sitting room and an hour or so with one of them would be very pleasant.

Bates met her on the stairs. 'Mr Royle has arrived, miss—he's in the drawing room.'

Annis stood staring at him, her mouth a little open. 'Mr Royle? What on earth . . . I didn't know Mrs Duvant was expecting him.' She suppressed the little spurt of excitement at the idea of meeting him again and reminded herself that she didn't like him, which made her voice sound reluctant.

'I suppose I'd better go . . .' her voice trailed off and Bates coughed gently. 'It would be a pity to disturb Mrs Duvant,' he reminded her.

Annis took a step down. 'Yes, of course, Bates.'

She went past him, crossed the hall, opened the drawing room door reluctantly and went unwillingly inside.

Jake Royle was standing, very much at home, before the fire. She said idiotically: 'Oh, hullo, Bates told me you were here. I'm afraid Mrs Duvant's having a nap, she always does after lunch.'

'Yes, I know that.' He smiled at her, and since it was obvious after a moment that he wasn't going to say anything else, she plunged into speech.

'Aren't you going back to New Zealand?' she asked.

His firm mouth twitched. 'Is that where you would consign me, Annis?'

'Of course not, Mr Royle. Why should I consign you anywhere?'

'My name is Jake.' He went on standing there, watching her and she sought feverishly for a topic of conversation. 'I'm staying with Mrs Duvant,' she said.

'Yes, I know that too.'

She frowned. At least he could give a hand with the conversation, the wretch! 'I expect you'll be staying for tea? I'm sure Mrs Duvant will want to see you.'

He grinned at her. 'I'm here for a few days—I visit Aunt Dora from time to time—we've known each other since I was a small boy,' and at the look of surprise on her face: 'Oh, she's not a genuine aunt, just an adopted one.'

'Oh, yes, I see. Perhaps you'd like to see your room?'

He answered her gravely enough, although his eyes danced with amusement.

'I expect Bates has taken my things upstairs for me. I'd love some tea—we can always have it again when Aunt Dora comes down.'

Annis, intent on being coolly impersonal, only succeeded in looking delightfully flustered as she rang the bell and rather belatedly asked if he would sit down, rather pink now at her lack of manners and a little cross because Jake seemed to have the power to make her feel shy and awkward, something which she, a parson's daughter, had learned not to be at an early age. And when tea came she was furious to find that her hands shook as she poured it. Jake, observing this, smiled to himself and embarked on a steady flow of small talk which was only interrupted by the arrival of Mrs Duvant, who came trotting in, her round face wreathed in smiles.

'Now isn't this nice?' she aked them. 'Annis, ring for more tea, will you? And I've left my spectacles somewhere ... Jake, I hope you can stay for a few days—you've got your car with you, I suppose? you can drive us ... Ah, thank you, dear, I knew I'd put them down somewhere.' She paused to pour tea. 'There's a concert at the Assembly Rooms this evening, will you come with us?'

Jake agreed lazily. 'Anything you say, Aunt Dora. I hope it's not Bach?'

'Strauss and Schubert and someone singing, but I can't remember the name.'

'As long as she's nice to look at.'

Annis, drinking her unwanted tea, wondered what on earth she should wear; the green or the blue velvet? She had nothing else, and if only she'd known she would have bought that blue crêpe dress, the one she had seen in Milsom Street; after all, she had her first week's money in her purse. Now it was too late. She knitted her brows; there was no earthly reason why she should fuss over what she should wear. What was good enough for her and Mrs Duvant was good enough for Jake Royle, it couldn't matter in the least to him what she wore. There would be dozens of pretty girls there, wearing gorgeous outfits. She became aware that they were both looking at her, Mrs Duvant smiling, Jake with his brows lifted in amusement. They must have said something.

'I'm sorry, did you ask me something?'

'No, love—I was just telling Jake what a delightful week we've had together.'

So why was Jake looking amused? Annis gave him a frosty look and offered him more cake.

She wore the green with the gold chain, and when she went downstairs it was a relief to find that Mrs

Duvant was wearing a plain wool dress, and although Jake had changed, the suit he had on was a conservative grey. She had to admit that it fitted him very well. So it should, considering what it had cost to have it made.

Dinner had a slightly festive air, partly due to the champagne Jake had brought with him, and partly owing to Mrs Duvant's high spirits. She was such a happy person it was impossible to be ill-tempered or miserable in her company.

They set off for the Assembly Rooms presently, in the best of spirits, driving through the rain-swept streets in Jake's Bentley, Mrs Duvant beside him wrapped in mink, and Annis behind, in her elderly winter coat. She was enjoying herself so much that she had quite forgotten that.

They sat with Mrs Duvant in between them and listened to the excellent orchestra, and later when the singer appeared, and turned out to be not only a very pretty woman but with a glorious voice, Annis couldn't stop herself from turning a little and peeping at Jake. He wasn't looking at the singer at all, but at her. He smiled before he looked away, leaving her with the feeling that although she didn't like him, she was becoming very aware of his charm.

When the concert was over they had a drink before going back to the house and she was nonplussed to find his manner towards her casual to the point of coolness; she must have imagined the warmth of that smile, and anyway, she told herself peevishly, why was she getting all worked up about it? She couldn't care less what he thought of her.

When they got back she waited merely to ask Mrs

Duvant if she needed her for anything before saying goodnight and going to her room. It had been a lovely evening, she told Mrs Duvant, and she had enjoyed herself very much. Her goodnight to Jake was brisk and delivered to his chin, since she wanted to avoid looking at him.

It would be a pity, she thought as she undressed, if he were to upset the gentle pattern of their days, but since he was to stay only a short time, that didn't really matter. She dismissed him from her thoughts and went to sleep, to dream, most infuriatingly, of him all night.

Mrs Duvant wasn't at breakfast the next morning, but Jake was. He was at table, reading the paper and making great inroads into eggs and bacon when Annis went down at her usual time. He got to his feet, wished her a friendly good morning, hoped that she had slept well, passed her the coffee pot and resumed his breakfast. Only good manners, she felt, prevented him from picking up his newspaper again.

Instead he carried on a desultory conversation, just sufficient to put her at her ease. Indeed, by the time their meal was finished, she found herself talking to him with something which amounted to pleasure.

'Aunt Dora wants to visit the American Museum this morning,' he told her as they left the room together. 'There's some embroidery exhibited there she intends to study. You'll be coming?' His voice was nicely casual.

'I expect so, Mrs Duvant likes someone with her, but perhaps if you're going there . . .'

He gave her a glance full of amused mockery. 'My

dear Annis, I know absolutely nothing about embroidery.'

She left him in the hall, wishing as she went upstairs that he was as nice as he had been at breakfast all the time, and not just when he felt like it. The way he looked at her with that horrid half-smile . . . She bounced into her room, dragged a comb ruthlessly through her hair, which didn't need it anyway, and went along to see how Mrs Duvant did. If it were possible, she would see if she could get out of going out that morning.

It wasn't possible. Mrs Duvant was so enthusiastic about the outing, pointing out how useful Annis was going to be, although Annis couldn't quite see why, that she didn't even suggest it. And as it turned out, Jake was charming, and once they got to the embroidery exhibition, wandered off on his own, leaving Mrs Duvant to exclaim over feather-stitching, smocking and the like while she made Annis write down a variety of notes which she thought might be useful to her later on.

It was during lunch that Jake observed that he would have to go back to London in two days' time. Annis was shocked at the keen disappointment she felt when he said it; she couldn't stand the sight of him—well, for most of the time anyway, but she would miss him. Which made it all the stranger that she hesitated about going downstairs again after she had tucked Mrs Duvant up for her post-prandial nap. But as she left Mrs Duvant's room she saw Jake disappearing out of the front door. She would be able to go downstairs and read by the fire in the small sitting room; she didn't want him to think that she was avoiding his company—that way if he thought about it at all, nor did she wish to bore him with her own company if he had a mind to be on his own. She found her book and curled up in one of the deep arm chairs drawn up to the cheerful fire.

She had read two pages when the door opened and Jake came in. 'Ah,' he said blandly, 'I had an idea you might have gone into hiding for the afternoon.'

A remark which instantly set her on edge. 'And why should you think that?' she wanted to know tartly. 'I have no reason to hide.'

'Oh, good, I can't help feeling that if we see more of each other we may eventually become friends. How about coming to dinner tomorrow evening? We'll go to Popjoy's and then go on somewhere to dance.'

A distressing vision of the blue velvet and the green jersey floated before Annis's eyes. She'd heard of Popjoy's, it was smart and expensive, and nothing would induce her to go there in either of these garments. With real regret she knew she would have to refuse, and the awful thing was that she actually had the money in her purse to buy that pretty blue crêpe she'd seen, only there was no time in which to buy it.

'That's awfully kind of you,' she said carefully, 'but I—I'm afraid I can't accept.'

'Why not?'

She sought for a good reason in a frenzy and couldn't think of one. Being a parson's daughter and the eldest, with a good example to set the others, she had been taught to speak the truth; only if it was going to hurt the hearer was it permissible to prevaricate. Well, she couldn't see that Jake was going to be hurt. If anyone was, it would be herself, having to admit that she had nothing to wear. She gave him a very direct look and explained: 'I haven't got a dress.' She had pinkened slightly in anticipation of his amusement, but she didn't look away.

Jake didn't smile, he said in a calm voice: 'That's a problem, but surely we can get round it? Have you got enough money to buy one?'

Strangely she didn't feel offended at the question. 'Well, yes—Mrs Duvant paid me, but you see I wouldn't have time to get to the shops.'

'Any particular shop?'

'Jolly's in Milsom Street.'

'I take it that if you did have a dress you'd come to dinner with me?' He wanted to know.

'I'd like to, that's if we could ... that is, if we wouldn't get on each other's nerves.'

He did smile then, but in such a friendly fashion that she smiled back. 'You never got on my nerves,' he assured her. 'Tell me, are you one of those women who take hours to buy something or could you find what you wanted in half an hour or so? Because if you could, we'll go now: I'll run you there in the car.'

Annis was out of her chair and making for the door. 'Give me five minutes!'

The dress was still there. She left Jake browsing in a book shop and went to try it on. The colour was becoming, a shade darker than her eyes, and the dress, although inexpensive, was quite well cut, made of some thick silky material with a chiffon ruffle outlining the neck and the cuffs. Examining heself in the fitting room, Annis decided that it would do very well; it could take the place of the blue velvet and that garment she could consign to the jumble sale. She didn't think it was quite the sort of dress Jake's girl-friends would wear, but since she wasn't one of them that didn't matter. She paid for it and on the way out spent most of the change on a pair of bronze sandals going cheap but nonetheless elegant.

Jake was still in the bookshop, but he picked up the armful of books he had bought when he saw her and took the dress box from her. 'Twenty minutes,' he remarked. 'Not bad. Did you find what you wanted?'

'Yes. I hope it'll do. We don't go out much at home and I don't often buy that kind of dress.'

Jake gave her a quick look. If the deplorable blue velvet had been anything to go by, he could not but agree with her. 'I'm sure it will be very charming,' he said comfortably. 'If you've got all you want, we'll go back. Aunt Dora will be wanting her tea.'

She was waiting for them, sitting in the small straightbacked chair she favoured, leafing through a pile of fashion magazines.

'Such a pity I'm all the wrong shape,' she greeted them. Her eyes fell on the dress box. 'You've been shopping—how delightful! Do let me see.'

'Since you're playing bridge tomorrow evening, Aunt Dora, I've asked Annis out to dinner.' Jake had strolled over to the fire with his back to Annis, busy undoing her purchase.

'Now that is a good idea,' enthused Mrs Duvant. 'Hold it up, dear.'

Annis did so, suddenly doubtful because in the splendidly furnished room with Mrs Duvant's wildly expensive outfit it looked what it was; a pretty inexpensive dress off the peg. But she was reassured at once by Mrs Duvant's warm admiration. 'Oh, very nice,' she declared, 'and such a lovely colour. Shoes?' She had glanced down at Annis's sensible low heels.

'Well, just as I was leaving the shop I saw these.' Annis produced the sandals and the two ladies examined them. 'They were going cheap and they'll be useful, because if I ever buy another dress, they'll go with almost anything.'

This ingenuous remark brought a smile to Jake's mouth; it was a very gentle smile and amused too. He had thought, when he first met Annis, that she was a bossy elder sister, prone to good works and with far too good an opinion of herself. That she was quite beautiful too, he had admitted without hesitation, but he hadn't quite believed her occasional dreaminess and her apparent contentment at the Rectory. Now he admitted that he had been quite wrong; she had made no effort to impress him— indeed, she had avoided him, she dealt with Mrs Duvant's endless small wants without as much as a frown, and he had been touched by her frank admission that she couldn't go out with him because she hadn't got a dress. He reflected ruefully that any of the girls he knew who had said that to him would have expected him to have taken them out and bought them one—and nothing off the peg either. He rather thought that if he had suggested to Annis that he would pay she would have thrown something at him. For all her sensible calmness he fancied that at times that red hair of hers might exert itself.

That evening after dinner they played poker, a game Annis had to be taught and which she picked up with ease, rather to Jake's surprise, until Mrs

Duvant remarked that it was only to be expected from a girl who had five A-levels to her credit, and one of these pure Maths. He just stopped himself asking her why she hadn't gone on to university, because of course, even with a grant, that would have cost money, and there were Edward and James to educate.

They played for high stakes, using the haricot beans Bates brought from the kitchen, and although Jake made a fortune in no time at all, Annis wasn't far behind him. Mrs Duvant, her black eyes snapping with pleasure, lost over and over again and when they at last called a halt, thanked heaven that she had been playing with beans and not money. But it had been good fun. Annis carefully gathered up the beans and returned them to Bates before going upstairs to bed with Mrs Duvant, leaving Jake by the fire, a briefcase of papers on the floor beside him, and a glass of whisky on the table.

The next morning Mrs Duvant announced that she had a wedding present to buy for a friend's daughter, and since Jake said that he had some work to do, she and Annis went to the shops together. It took almost all the morning, trying to decide between table linen and silver tea knives. In the end Mrs Duvant, never one to cavil over money, bought both.

And after lunch Jake went back to his work and since Mrs Duvant had retired for her usual nap, Annis got into her outdoor things and went for a walk in the park. It was a chilly, blustery day and somehow it suited her mood; she was feeling vaguely restless, but she couldn't think why. Everything was all right at home; she had a letter that morning, in another day or two there would be forty pounds in her pocket and she had no worries. She came to the conclusion that Jake's visit had unsettled her. She had never met anyone like him before; Matt she had grown up with and treated much as she treated her brothers, but Jake made her feel selfconscious and shy, although she had to admit that she was beginning to enjoy his company. She marched briskly into the teeth of the wind and went back presently, her face rosy with fresh air and with a splendid appetite for her tea.

Seen under the soft lighting of her bedroom the blue crêpe looked nice; so did the sandals. It was a pity that she had to wear her winter coat, but she didn't suppose that would matter overmuch; no one would see it. She went downstairs with it over her arm, admiring the sandals as she went.

'Very nice,' declared Jake from the hall. 'Stunning, in fact. What's more, you're beautifully prompt.'

He was in the clerical grey again, looking older and very assured. Looking at him, Annis felt sure that the evening would go without a hitch; he would be a man able to get the best table in the restaurant and instant attention. She said thank you rather shyly and went to say goodnight to Mrs Duvant.

She had been quite right, she told herself as she got ready for bed in the early hours of the next morning; the evening had been one to remember, for her at any rate—although it seemed likely that Jake had spent so many similar evenings with other, more interesting companions, that he would probably forget it at once.

Popjoys was the kind of place she had read about

in the *Harpers* Mrs Avery occasionally lent her. In a Beau Nash house where its guests drank their aperitifs in the elegant drawing-room before going to the equally elegant dining room, it was a world she had never expected to enter. They had eaten mousseline of salmon, spiced chicken with apricots and finished with chocolate soufflé, and just as she had guessed, they had a well placed table for two and the proprietor had welcomed them warmly, conjuring up wine waiter and waiter and recommending the best dishes. Her mouth watered at the thought of the salmon. The wine had been nice too; she had almost no knowledge of wines and beyond Jake's careless: 'I think we'll drink hock, shall we?' he didn't bother her about it. She drank what was in her glass and found it delicious. By the time dinner was finished she felt very happy about everything, and when Jake suggested that they might dance somewhere for an hour or two she had agreed very readily. Her sleepy head on the pillow, she couldn't quite remember where they had gone; an hotel in the town, although she hadn't noticed its name. They had had a table there too and Jake had ordered some wine, but they had got up to dance before it was brought and since the floor wasn't crowded and the band was good they went on dancing for quite some time.

Back at the table they talked, but there again she couldn't remember what they had said, only that it had been pleasant and they had laughed a good deal. She sat up in bed suddenly. Perhaps she had drunk too much and made a fool of herself, but she couldn't have been too bad, because they had gone on dancing for a long time before getting into the car and coming back. The combined pleasure of the evening lulled her to sleep; she was on the very edge of it when she started awake. With vivid clarity she remembered kissing Jake goodnight in the hall. True, he had kissed her first but she need not have kissed him back with quite such fervour. At the time it had seemed a perfectly natural thing to do, but now she wasn't so sure; when she got back home to the Rectory she was going to remember it with hideous embarrassment. And pleasure, a small voice at the back of her head persisted.

CHAPTER THREE

ANNIS took as long as she possibly could to dress in the morning. She would have to meet Jake sooner or later, but she wanted it to be later. Her cheeks grew red each time she thought of the previous evening, but awkward or not, she would have to go down to breakfast and there wasn't much use being cowardly about it. She marched downstairs and went into the dining-room, to find it empty, and when Bates came in with the coffee pot he informed her that Mr Royle had already left for London.

Quite unreasonably, she was instantly furious. Jake might at least have left a message, told her the evening before, given some hint that he wouldn't be seeing her again. She ate without appetite and was hard put to it to be cheerful when Mrs Duvant came down presently, wanting to know if she had enjoyed her evening with Jake, where they had been, what they had done, and what a pity it was that he had had to go back to London. 'Though I daresay we'll see something of him before you go back home, dear.'

Annis said: 'Oh, yes—how nice,' and hoped with her whole heart that she'd never see him again. At the same time she felt such a wave of regret at the very idea that she was quite bewildered.

'Of course,' went on Mrs Duvant, at her most gossipy, 'he had so many friends that every moment of his leisure is filled, and he doesn't have much leisure, I can tell you. And all the girls are after him, and who can blame them? He's quite something to look at, isn't he? and with more money than he knows what to do with and not married.' She shot a quick glance at Annis, sitting quietly unravelling Mrs Duvant's endless knitting. 'I thought at first that you didn't hit it off together, but perhaps I was wrong.'

Annis answered guardedly: 'We haven't much in common, Mrs Duvant, and I rather think that Jake asked me out just by way of filling in an evening. I enjoyed it, though.' Especially being kissed at the end of it, she added silently. She would have to forget that, of course, but no doubt in a few weeks' time, when she was home again, it would all seem like a dream, and dreams had a habit of fading. She gave the knitting a vicious tug and sat up straight. Besides, she still didn't like him; he was far too sure of himself, and if he had thought for one single minute that she was going to be like all those other girls and make a play for him, then he was going to be sadly disappointed . . . She ripped out a row of stitches that had nothing wrong with them at all and had to knit the whole lot again.

It was a good thing that Mrs Duvant had an urge to go shopping, so that the morning and a good deal of the afternoon was taken up with this agreeable pastime, and in the evening there was a film which she particularly wanted to see.

She was a tireless little woman. One day succeeded another and on each of them she discovered something different to do, and when they weren't somewhere, guide book in hand, they were at the house, discussing new curtains and covers and whether it would be a good idea to have the hall close-carpeted over the polished wood blocks. All in all, the days were filled from morning until bedtime and Annis had little time to feel even faintly regretful of the few days of Jake's company.

It seemed to her that Mrs Duvant was doing too much, and rather hesitantly she said so.

'Nonsense, my dear,' said that lady cheerfully. 'I'm not one to sit around in a chair and wait to grow old.' She chuckled. 'Well, I'm that already, aren't I?'

'Of course you're not, only you look thinner, Mrs Duvant—do you suppose you should rest a little more? Perhaps an hour before dinner each evening?'

'Certainly not, Annis. What a waste of time that would be! There's that play we simply must see and the concerts at the Assembly Rooms, and I've promised to play bridge at least once a week. No, dear, I'm very happy as I am. Now let me see, where was it we saw that velvet I thought might do for the new curtains?'

So Annis said no more, although she still felt uneasy.

And two days later she knew she had been right They had just sat down to their dinner when Mrs Duvant said in an urgent voice: 'Annis, I feel ill . . .'

Annis took one look at the grey face opposite her and got out of her chair. Mrs Duvant looked awful, but Annis wasn't the eldest of six, all prone to accident or illness from time to time, for nothing. She scooped up Mrs Duvant from her chair and carried her carefully across the hall, meeting an astonished Bates on the way.

'Open the sitting-room door, will you, Bates, and telephone the doctor to come at once. Mrs Duvant isn't well!'

She laid her burden down on one of the sofas in the room, put a cushion under her head and felt for her pulse.

'I'm not dead yet,' whispered Mrs Duvant, opening one eye.

'Of course you're not,' agreed Annis bracingly and wishing Mrs Duvant wasn't such a frightful colour. 'I've asked the doctor to come, though, just to take a look—you may have been doing too much, you know.'

'Impossible,' whispered Mrs Duvant, and smiled tiredly.

Mrs Bates had joined them silently and Annis asked her to get Mrs Duvant's bed ready. 'Because I'm sure the doctor will want her to rest for a day or two. Can you think of anything else we should do?'

Mrs Bates shook her head and went away, and after a moment Mrs Duvant said more strongly: 'Telephone Jake—tell him to come, he'll understand.'

'When the doctor's been,' suggested Annis gently.

'No, now.' She gave the ghost of a chuckle. 'It's all right, I shan't go away.'

So Annis went across to the telephone and looked up Jake's number in the elegant leather book on the table and dialled it. His voice, deep and decisive, answered almost at once.

'Mrs Duvant asked me to phone you; she isn't

well, we're waiting for the doctor. She would like you to come.'

He didn't ask any questions, although she had expected him to, even to suggest that he should wait until the morning. 'Tell her I'm now on my way,' he said abruptly, and hung up.

The doctor, when he came, which was within minutes of Bates's phone call, wouldn't hear of Mrs Duvant being moved for the moment, and rather to Annis's surprise he didn't do much; he took his patient's pulse, her blood pressure, peered into her eyes and then said rallyingly: 'I warned you, Dora, you've been burning the candle at both ends and they're on the point of meeting.'

'Oh, pooh,' said Mrs Duvant in a voice which was a shadow of its usual strength. 'I told you I was going to do as I liked.'

'And now I'm going to do what I like,' observed the doctor firmly. 'You're going to have an injection, just enough to take away the pain and give us a chance to get you comfortable and into your bed.' He glanced at Annis. 'If you would be so good as to hold Mrs Duvant's arm steady.'

Mrs Duvant's eyes closed within minutes. 'I'll carry her upstairs, perhaps you and Mrs Bates can get her undressed?'

Annis nodded. 'Is Mrs Duvant very ill?' she asked.

He looked surprised for a moment. 'She's dying. She's had cancer for some months now; I've nursed her along, but we both knew that she wouldn't have long. You didn't know?'

Annis shook her head. 'No. Should anyone be told? She asked me to ring her godson, and he's on his way. She has a brother . . .'

'Colonel Avery—yes, let him know, will you. Are you a member of the family?'

'No, my parents are friends of the Averys'. I'm here as companion to Mrs Duvant for a few weeks while she settles in here.' Her hands were shaking and she put them behind herself longing for Jake to come.

Between them, she and Mrs Bates got Mrs Duvant into bed, and although she roused a little as they did so, she dozed off once more and didn't wake when the doctor came to take another look at her.

'She should sleep for a while,' he told Annis. 'I have another urgent visit to pay, but I'll be back. Can you manage or shall I try and get a nurse?'

'I can manage, and Bates and Mrs Bates are very good. Is there anything I should do? Will she be in pain?'

'She won't rouse for another two hours at least, possibly longer, and I'll be back by then; if you're worried about her let me know at once and I'll come.'

The house was very quiet after he had gone. Bates crept in with a tray on which there was a bowl of soup and had put it down on the table by Annis's chair. 'Just take this, miss,' he urged. 'The night's going to be a long one.'

She thanked him, urged him to see that both he and Mrs Bates had something to eat too, and warned him that Jake would be coming—a piece of information which Bates received with relieved satisfaction.

'Me and Mrs Bates, we knew that the mistress

had had bad turns from time to time; Mr Jake warned us of that, but we never expected anything like this, miss.'

He looked so shocked and upset that Annis got up and went to put a hand on his shoulder. 'Perhaps it won't be as bad as it looks,' she said, knowing how empty her words were and that neither of them believed them, anyway.

Bates came back presently to fetch the tray and ask anxiously if there was any change and when might Colonel Avery be expected. 'Because he'll need to stay the night, miss,' he reminded her.

'Yes, of course—I'm sorry, Bates, I forgot to tell you that Colonel and Mrs Avery were out, so was Matthew. I left a message and asked that they should get it at the first possible moment, but they'd gone to some friends for dinner, and unfortunately no one knew who they were. I expect it will take a little time to find them.' Annis glanced at the clock. 'It's only ten o'clock, though, they're bound to telephone as soon as they hear.'

'Yes, of course, miss. What a blessing that you're here, miss. Mrs Bates asks if she should sit here for a bit.'

'How kind of her! But I'm all right and the doctor's coming back round about midnight. I thought I'd stay here until he comes, perhaps he'll know more by then.'

There was no sound in the room when Bates had gone save the faint ticking of the clock and the even fainter sound of Mrs Duvant's breathing. Annis pulled her chair a little nearer the bed just in case its occupant should wake, and composed herself to wait.

Half an hour later the door was softly opened and Jake came in. Annis turned her head and looked at him, not speaking. He looked as calm and unruffled as he always did, immaculate in a dinner jacket, bringing with him the strong feeling that he would be able to cope with anything no matter how awkward the situation.

He said, 'Hullo, Annis,' in a quiet voice and went past her to the bed. 'The doctor's been?'

'Yes, at about half past eight. He's coming again before midnight. I'm to ring him if it's necessary.'

His eyes examined her pale face. 'I see.' He didn't say anything else until Bates, who had followed him in, had put down a tray of coffee on one of the tables and gone again, then he poured for them both, added brandy to both cups and brought one over to her. 'Drink that, and tell me what's happened.'

The brandy warmed her cold insides and the coffee cleared her head. She gave a succinct account of the evening without adding any comments of her own, and any doubts she had had about doing the right thing were dispelled by his quiet, 'You've been splendid.'

He refilled her cup and drew up another chair on the other side of the bed, and presently when Mrs Duvant opened her eyes and said in a quite strong voice: 'How long have you been here, Jake?' he answered her in a perfectly normal voice. 'Twenty minutes ago, my dear.'

'Had to leave a date, did you?' she chuckled, and it was like dry leaves rustling.

'I did; a delectable blonde who turned into a flaming virago when I stood her up.' He picked up a hand lying on the silk coverlet and kissed it. 'You're worth a roomful of blondes, but I've told you that before.'

Mrs Duvant smiled at him. 'We've had some good times together. I didn't have any children, but now it's like having a son and a daughter with me.' She turned her head and looked at Annis. 'You make a darling daughter, my dear—one day you'll make some lucky man a darling wife.'

'Why, thank you.' Annis managed a perfectly natural smile, taking her cue from Jake, although there was a lump in her throat fit to choke her. 'I think you'd make a lovely mum——' She paused as the door bell sounded faintly and Bates's elderly voice spoke to someone downstairs—the doctor.

The two men shook hands and the doctor said: 'You made good time, Jake, not much on the roads.'

'Hardly a thing. Do you want us out of the way while you talk to Aunt Dora?'

'No, that won't be necessary.' He bent over the bed, taking Mrs Duvant's pulse and then her blood pressure. 'I'm going to give you another injection,' he told her. 'The pain's starting up again, isn't it?'

She nodded. 'I should have loved to have talked to Jake, we've only had a few minutes.'

'I'll be here when you wake up, darling,' said Jake from the window, and turned to give her a grin. 'I'll stay here and nod off in a chair and we'll have a cup of tea together.'

'And Annis?'

'She'll be here too. I'll take a few days off next week and we'll play poker.'

Mrs Duvant smiled slowly and allowed Annis to

lift her arm for the doctor to give the injection. 'I'll
look forward to it,' she answered him a voice hardly
to be heard now.

She drifted off without speaking again, and presently the doctor went and Jake went with him. He
was back again in a very few minutes, though, to sit
down again opposite Annis. 'Bates is bringing up a
pot of tea,' he told her, and at her look: 'That's
what Aunt Dora would like.'

'I'm sorry' she felt her cheeks grow warm, 'that
was silly of me.' And when the tea came she meekly
accepted a cup. It had the effect of dissolving the
lump in her throat so that, quite against her will,
tears began to pour down her cheeks.

Jake crossed the room and took the cup from her
and pulled her gently out of her chair. 'Now look,
darling, you must stop crying. Aunt Dora wouldn't
like it, for one thing, nor do I for another.' He put
an arm round her shoulders and held her close; she
could feel his immense vitality wrapped round her
like a cloak and felt instantly better.

'So sorry,' she managed.

'No, don't be sorry for a warm heart, Annis—
there are enough cold ones around.' He fished
a handkerchief out of a pocket and started to
mop her face. 'That's better. Do you think you
can go on for a bit? It won't be for much
longer.'

She stared up at him. 'Isn't Mrs Duvant . . . You
said we'd all have a cup of tea . . .'

'So I did. You're not very grown up, are you,
darling?' He kissed the top of her head a small ges-
ture which did much to comfort her, and went on: 'I
think—I know that Aunt Dora would like it if we

were to stay here with her, but if you feel you can't she'd understand.'

'I'll stay.' Annis leaned away from him and he dropped his arms at once.

'That's my girl! Sit down again and finish that tea and I'll tell you about Aunt Dora. She's had a most interesting life, you know.'

He rambled on quietly, sitting by the bed, a small limp hand in his, talking about Mrs Duvant's travels, which had been numerous, and all the things she had done without the approval of her relations. 'She had a splendid life, and she and her husband adored each other; when he died she disappeared for several months—trekked through darkest Africa, or was it America?'

His gentle musings, needing no reply, gave Annis time to pull herself together, and when after a little while he said: 'Well, it's over, my dear,' she said quite calmly: 'What do we do now? How can I help?'

And then she went to the bed and knelt down like a child for a few moments, then got to her feet and stood looking down on the quiet face. 'She lived until the last minute, didn't she? I mean, so many elderly people start dying slowly years before they need to.'

Jake had his back to her, looking out into the night. 'You've hit the nail on the head, bless you. I'll phone the doctor, and will you see if the Bates's are still up?'

The remainder of the night passed in a blur of happenings: the Colonel arriving, the doctor, Mrs Bates whisking her off to bed . . . Annis woke late, astonished that she had slept.

Everyone was at breakfast when she got down—

Jake and the Colonel, Mrs Avery and Matt. They bade her a cheerful good morning and the Colonel asked at once if she would like to go back with them later in the morning.

Annis, without realising it, looked at Jake.

'I'd like you to stay, Annis, I'll need some help, and there are some things the Bates's can't do.'

Mrs Avery said crossly: 'It's a great pity that we can't stay, but we can't put off the Lord Lieutenant . . .' She shot a glance at Matt, stolidly working his way through a good breakfast. 'Matt, surely you could stay?'

'But why, Mother? Jake can cope with everything, you know that, and Annis can manage perfectly well.'

His mother said even more crossly, seeing her matrimonial plans sliding away before they'd even got going: 'You and Annis have always done everything together . . .'

'But, Mother, we're not children any more.'

Annis, playing around with a bit of toast, held her tongue, while Jake sat back at his ease, drinking his coffee, smiling just a little.

But he looked perfectly grave when Mrs Avery turned to him. 'Matt's right,' he told her soothingly, 'there's not much he could do, as long as Colonel Avery doesn't mind me getting on with things . . .'

Colonel Avery surfaced from toast and marmalade. 'Of course not, dear boy. After all, you're one of the executors, and I must get back . . .'

'Of course.' Jake was at his most bland. 'If anything comes up, I'll phone you.'

And so the Averys went away again presently, and Jake took Annis by the arm and marched her into the sitting-room. 'Sit down quietly,' he told her, 'and read the papers. I'll join you for coffee presently.'

'Yes, but isn't there something I should do?'

'Not for a little while,' he told her gently.

So she pretended to read the news while she listened to quiet feet going up and downstairs and the murmur of voices, and then Jake's firm footfall crossing the hall and going into the drawing-room.

Half an hour later he joined her. 'It's just occurred to me—shouldn't you ring your family? Will your mother object to you staying here?'

'Of course not. Not if I can be of some use . . . but I'll ring her, if you don't mind.'

He nodded. 'The funeral is in four days' time. I'll stay until then, and I hope you will too. This afternoon, if you feel you can, I want you to sort through Aunt Dora's jewellery. I know about her will, of course, she's left a good deal of it to members of the family, and it would help a lot if you could check it.'

'Are there a lot of nephews and nieces?'

'Dozens. Matt will get quite a nice little legacy, she was fond of him.'

He looked at her as he spoke, but her face showed no interest at this news.

'It will come in handy when he marries,' persisted Jake.

'Yes, I expect it will; is there anything I can do?'

'Yes, come for a brisk walk with me.'

Which they did, through Royal Victoria Park, the Botanical Gardens and across High Common. It was a fine morning, still cold but right for walking, and they arrived back more than ready for their lunch.

The afternoon passed quickly. There was an astonishing amount of jewellery to sort through and they did it together in front of the sitting room fire, while Jake talked about Aunt Dora, so naturally that it seemed as though she wasn't dead at all, and when Annis remarked on this he said briskly: 'Well, in a way, she isn't, and I for one don't believe in hushed voices and drawn blinds and nor did she.'

They ate their dinner on the best of terms and afterwards Jake went away to do some more telephoning. When he joined her by the fire in the sitting-room presently, he observed: 'How pleasant, just like an old married couple.'

He didn't seem to expect a reply, which was just as well, as she couldn't think of one, but sat down opposite her and picked up a newspaper.

Five minutes passed. 'How dull,' observed Annis thoughtfully.

Jake lowered his newspaper. 'What's how dull?'

'Being an old married couple.' She glanced up at him and then went back to her knitting.

'Now let us go into this in some depth.' He put the paper down and stretched out in his chair. 'I should imagine that after the hurly-burly of years of married life, it must be very pleasant to share your fireside and your declining years with someone you've loved and still love.'

'That sounds too good to be true.'

'No, it's not. I for one intend to make it true.'

Annis dropped a stitch. 'Oh? Are you thinking of getting married?'

'I've got past the thinking stage. I now know I am.'

'How—how nice.' It was ridiculous to feel so forlorn about it. Annis knitted fiercely, making a botch of the pattern, reminding herself that she didn't like him, after all—arrogant, too self-assured, more money than was good for him, far too good-looking, and all these quite drowned out by a persistent little voice at the back of her head reminding her that he could, when he wished, be kind and thoughtful and amusing and always knew what had to be done without being bossy about it.

'And you?' went on Jake. 'Do you and Matt intend to marry?'

She dropped several stitches. 'Me and Matt? Get married? Whatever do you mean? We grew up together.'

'Some people would say that was an excellent basis for a successful marriage.'

'Pooh, what utter nonsense! I can't imagine anything more dull—besides, Matt's only a boy.'

Jake settled further into his chair. 'Do you mind if I smoke?' and when he had got his pipe going: 'So he's not your ideal husband?'

'You must be joking!' Annis let her work fall into her lap and went on dreamily: 'Someone who doesn't expect me to go out in all weathers and notices if I've got something new on.' She paused. 'Though I can't blame Matt for that, because I don't have many new clothes for him to notice.' She stared at the wall opposite her, quite forgetful of her companion. 'Always polite and never shouting me down, considerate of my every wish, noticing if I've got a headache, remembering anniversaries with red roses . . .' She stopped because Jake was laughing at her. She said huffily: 'You would laugh!'

'Darling, you're such a child and yet you're a

practical young woman too—a delightful mixture.'

Annis frowned. 'Don't call me darling, that's the third time. It doesn't mean anything, not—when you say it like that.'

He said very softly: 'No? Well, you can make what you like of that, Annis.'

A remark which kept her silent for quite some time, trying to decide just what he meant; or perhaps he hadn't meant anything at all. That was why she didn't like him, she told herself, because she was never quite sure if he meant what he said.

But during the next few days she found herself forgetting more and more often that she didn't like him. He was a good companion, and what was more, he kept her busy helping him with the hundred and one small tasks which had to be done, and each afternoon, whatever the weather, he marched her off for a long walk so that she began to look like her old self again. He expected her to help with the arrangements for the funeral too, treating the whole thing with a matter-of-fact air which robbed it of too much solemnity, and made it easy for her to greet the host of relations and friends who arrived. Her mother and father came at the same time as Colonel and Mrs Avery and Matt, and Mrs Avery, hoping to take advantage of the circumstances, did her best to throw Matt and Annis together on every possible occasion. She had no success at all. Annis had too much to do and Matt, after a perfunctory 'Hullo, old girl,' had made a beeline for a cluster of pretty cousins he hadn't seen for some time.

It was when almost everyone had gone again and only a handful of family were left that Mrs Avery broached the subject of Annis going back with Matt.

'We came in his car,' she pointed out, 'and he'll be glad of your company—I expect you want to get home as soon as possible, Annis.'

Annis, poised at the door with a tray load of cups and saucers for the Bates to wash up, stood very still, it had struck her forcibly and in utter surprise that she had no wish to go home. She loved her parents dearly and she had no objection to Matt but she wanted to stay where she was until the last possible moment. And the reason for that was standing across the room from her, talking to her father: Jake, looking even more self-assured than usual, very much in command of the occasion and to all intents and purposes unaware of her existence.

She took a firmer grip of the tray; now was not the time to discover that she was in love with him. How much more convenient if she could have made the discovery in the peace and quiet of her own room without Mrs Avery's keen eye boring holes in her back. And her mother, bless her, had turned round to hear her answer, too.

The first one to speak was Jake. 'Oh, I'm sure you won't mind if Annis stays for another day or two. Mrs Fothergill, will you be an angel and allow me to bring her back, say, the day after tomorrow? There's still quite a lot of tidying away and clearing up to do and she's been so useful.'

It would have been hard to have refused, and anyway, her mother liked him. She said now: 'Well, of course, Jake, if Annis doesn't mind. I'm glad she can be of help at such a difficult time. And you'll bring her back?'

'With pleasure, and many thanks.' He glanced at

Annis. 'You won't mind, darling?' he asked deliberately.

Annis felt her cheeks glowing like hot coals. The wretch, with his beastly little mocking smile! She didn't love him at all, she hated him. She said coldly: 'If I can help, I'll stay,' and sailed through the door with her tray.

When she got back, her cheeks cool once more, everyone was getting ready to leave. She kissed Mrs Avery's cross face, dutifully hugged her mother and father, said goodbye to Matt and the Colonel, and waved them away from the doorstep, with Jake standing beside her for all the world as though he owned the place.

Which, she was to discover, he did. She hadn't been present at the reading of the will, nor was she particularly interested. From the remarks she had overheard from various members of the family, Mrs Duvant had been more than generous. It was only as they stood in the hall once more that she asked, anxious to fill the silence between them: 'Do you have to put the house up for sale? Do you want an inventory made?'

'Lord, no. I've no intention of selling it, I like it too much. I shall keep the Bates's on, of course, and come down whenever I can.'

Annis stopped her walk to the drawing-room and turned to look at him. 'You mean it's yours? This house?'

'Don't look so shocked! Don't you think I'll look nice living in it? Conjure up a picture in your romantic mind of me, surrounded by the wife of my choice and an assortment of kids.'

He leaned against a console table, his hands in his

pockets, smiling at her, and because she had a vivid imagination anyway, she did just that to such good purpose that she felt tears filling her eyes and with a quite unintelligible mutter she turned and ran upstairs to her room.

She stayed there, pleading a severe headache, and although she was famished, made do with a tray of thin soup which Mrs Bates brought up during the evening. What with hunger and misery, she had a poor night.

CHAPTER FOUR

THERE had been time, during the hours she had lain awake, for Annis to pull herself together. By the time she went downstairs to breakfast the following morning, she felt able to cope with any situation which might arise, so it was with a distinct feeling of being let down that she sat down to table, for Jake greeted her in a casual manner which put her strongly in mind of her brothers and beyond a few brief observations about the weather and the news, had nothing much to say to her.

She ate dreamily, imagining what it would be like to be married to Jake and eat breakfast with him every morning of her life, only he'd have to talk to her, not sit buried behind the *Financial Times*. But dreaming was a waste of time, especially about him. She said loudly: 'What would you like me to do? You said yesterday that there was still some clearing up to be done.'

He lowered the paper and studied her. 'Now I wonder what I've done—or not done. You look as though your hair is going to burst into flames at any minute. Did I really say that? I couldn't have been thinking. Half an hour's telephoning should see the finish of our day's chores. I thought we might take a run into the country.'

Annis was quite unable to stop the smile spreading across her pretty face. 'Oh, that would be super!' She didn't dare say any more or he might be put off by too much enthusiasm. 'Are you quite sure there's nothing more to do?' she wanted to know.

'Quite sure. I'll go and do my phoning now and you can tell Mrs Bates that we won't be back until the evening, ask her to arrange a dinner which won't spoil if we're a bit late.'

'Where on earth are we going?' She looked down at her tweed skirt and sweater. 'Will I do as I am?'

Jake said gravely, his eyes dancing, 'You'll do very nicely, Annis,' and went away, leaving her to drink her last cup of coffee and hurry along to the kitchen to see Mrs Bates.

It wasn't until they were leaving Bath behind that Annis asked: 'Where are we going?'

'Oxfordshire, on the edge of the Cotswolds—a village called Minster Lovell.' She waited for him to say more, but he didn't, so she asked: 'Why?'

'It's my home—I have a family, you know.' He shot her a sideways glance. 'Why do you look surprised?'

'Well, you—that is, you don't seem the kind of man to have a family.' She went a little pink. 'I don't mean to be rude, but it's hard to explain.'

'Ah, you mean a lone wolf with no one to cut him down to size and only himself to bother about.'

'No, I didn't mean that at all.' She didn't know what she meant. She longed to be able to put into words what she felt about him. 'I can't explain, I don't know how.'

He went on talking just as though she hadn't spoken. 'Minster Lovell is a charming place, I think you'll like it. Not quite Cotswolds but near enough,

I've always thought. We'll stop in Cirencester for coffee.'

He stopped at the King's Head in Market Place and kept up a casual flow of amusing small talk while they had their coffee before going on again. The day was fine and clear and the country around them delightful in the thin sunshine; Annis began to enjoy herself. She had expected to feel awkward in Jake's company now that she knew that she loved him, but she felt no such thing—indeed, she was dreading the moment when he and she would part company.

He had taken the road through Burford and before they got to Witney turned off to the north to where Minster Lovell lay, nicely hidden from the rest of the world with the river Windrush woven into its heart.

Jake drove over the bridge at the beginning of the village, along its street and up the slight incline at the farther end. Here the houses were rather grand, their walls of Burford stone, and stone-tiled too. He turned in at the gates of one of these houses, standing solitary overlooking the village, and stopped the car in the small semi-circular drive. In summer it would be pretty with roses and Virginia creeper and clematis. Now it was rather bare, with a few early daffodils poking up reluctant heads. The house was of Burford stone, like the others, with a steep pitched roof and a great many gables and small casement windows. It had a sturdy front door that was opened as they got out of the car.

The woman standing there was elderly, tall and boney and fierce-looking, and when Jake called out: 'Hullo, Poppy, lovely to see you,' Annis thought what a very inappropriate name she had.

The rather craggy face softened as Poppy opened the door wider 'Well, it's nice to see you, Mr Jake.' Her eyes slid past him to Annis. 'And the young lady.'

'Miss Annis Fothergill—meet Poppy, family friend and general mainstay.' He kissed Poppy and then kissed Annis, and at her look and heightened colour, 'Just to even things up,' he explained.

There was a narrow hall that widened into a square room which had several doors in its walls as well as two passages leading from it and a carved wood staircase, it was furnished simply with wall tables, upon which were bowls laden with spring flowers, a pair of carved wooden chairs, and a Gothic oak chest, worn smooth with age. The floor was gleaming oak too, half covered by a faded but still beautiful needlework carpet.

One of the doors was partly open. Jake pushed it wider and propelled Annis gently through it, into a low-ceilinged room, light and airy and agreeably furnished with chintz-covered chairs, several small tables, a mahogany break-fronted bookcase with glazed doors, and a large velvet-covered sofa. The sash window was curtained with mushroom velvet, and the carpet was the same colour; a restful room as well as being very pretty.

The same adjectives could be applied to the lady who got out of one of the chairs and came towards them. She was small and plump, her grey hair elegantly dressed, her round, merry face nicely made up. Her eyes were blue and twinkly and she was smiling widely. Hard on her heels came an elderly man who could have been no one else but Jake's father. Annis thought with a little flair of temper, Jake could have told me . . . But the thought was swallowed up in the little lady's warm greeting. She was made to feel at home instantly, kissed heartily first by Jake's mother, then his father, and then finally and for no apparent reason by Jake. Twice in ten minutes, she thought, and blushed, because she had liked it.

'Well, isn't this nice?' Mrs Royle wanted to know of no one in particular, and tucked an arm through Annis's. 'You come and sit with me, dear—there's time for a drink before lunch and I want to hear all about you.'

'But there isn't anything to tell,' protested Annis, and then found herself, a glass of sherry in one hand, answering the questions her companion lost no time in putting to her. By the time Poppy came to the door to tell them that lunch was ready, she reckoned that Mrs Royle had a very good idea of her family and background and, strangely, she didn't mind: the questions had been put so kindly.

Jake had got to his feet and gone out of the room behind Poppy, to return within a minute or two, his arm tucked into that of a very old, very small lady, dressed with great elegance in black, her white hair waved in the style of the thirties: she looked frail, but there was nothing frail about her voice.

'Ah, there she is, and just as pretty as you said: quite a beauty, in fact. I hope she likes children?' She had come to a standstill and Annis realised that she was waiting for her to go to her. She advanced willingly, quite composed though a trifle bewildered by the old lady's remarks. Was she being vetted for a governess's post? she wondered. Jake might have thought she would welcome a job after working for Mrs Duvant. She shook the small bony hand carefully and smiled down at the old lady.

'I'm Jake's grandmother. I seldom come down to lunch, but I wanted to meet you. I like your name and I like you, my dear—there's plenty of you and you look healthy.'

Annis pinkened slightly, aware of Jake's dark eyes on her face. She said a little breathlessly: 'Yes, I'm always very well, thank you.'

The old lady nodded to herself and then looked up at her grandson.

'Well, you took your time,' she told him, 'and a good thing too as far as I can see.' She added with a faintly peevish air: 'Where's lunch? I'm hungry.'

Her son and daughter-in-law had listened to her without comment, now they assured her soothingly that lunch was on the table and there was no reason to wait a minute longer. They all crossed the hall into a smaller room with a round table at its centre, a thick brown carpet and apricot-coloured curtains, adding a splash of colour to the cream walls. A restful room, thought Annis, and sat herself down where she was bidden—opposite Jake. She would have preferred another place, away from his frequent dark glance, but she was a sensible girl and she was hungry. She ate a delicious meal, taking care not to catch his eye. Not too difficult as it turned out, for the conversation was general with old Mrs Royle taking more than her share of it. But she made no more reference to Annis, only showing a lively interest in her grandson and his work.

'Made your million yet?' she wanted to know with a chuckle. 'How's that factory in New Zealand?'

'Coming along nicely, Grandmother.' Jake's saturnine face broke into a smile. 'How about coming with me next time I visit it?'

'Take care I don't,' she answered. 'You'll have other company with you, I've no doubt, and I've no wish to play gooseberry.'

Did that mean, thought Annis bleakly, that he had a girl-friend, that he was going to marry? She turned a polite ear to Mrs Royle's gentle chat about the garden while she pondered the matter, and came to the conclusion that probably he had.

They went back to the drawing-room for their coffee and old Mrs Royle was led back again upstairs where she had her own rooms. Annis found herself sitting beside Mrs Royle while that lady rambled pleasantly from fashion to housekeeping and back again. But not for long. Jake came back, refused coffee and pulled her to her feet. 'Come and see the garden,' he suggested. 'Father's already asleep and Mother always has a nap after lunch.'

True, Mr Royle was sitting back in his chair, his mouth slightly open, his eyes shut. Any moment now he was going to snore. But Mrs Royle didn't look in the least sleepy, although she laughed and nodded at Jake. 'And get a wrap for Annis,' she begged. 'It's cold outside.'

They went out through a small side door, Annis swathed in an old Burberry from a miscellaneous collection of coats hanging in the passage; they reminded her of home, and made her feel a little homesick until Jake took her arm and walked briskly down a brick path towards a shrubbery at the far end.

He said unexpectedly: 'I'll take you home tomorrow.'

'Oh—yes, of course. Thank you very much.' The

words sounded silly, but she had been taken by surprise.

He spoke again and now his voice was very smooth and faintly amused. 'Grandmother approves of you, isn't that nice? She longs to be a great-granny.'

Annis gave him a puzzled look and stopped walking. 'Whatever has that got to do with me?' she wanted to know.

'I told her that I was going to marry you'. He sounded so casual that she could only gape at him. 'You what?' she managed.

'Told her that I was going to marry you,' he repeated patiently. 'I daresay,' he went on thoughtfully, 'I might not have mentioned it for a few days, but she rather precipitated things.'

'But I don't . . . you don't . . . we don't know each other, we're not even friends.'

'No? I thought we were. Granted, initially we may not have taken to each other, but having got to know you, I fancy that you're just the wife I'm looking for.' He went on deliberately: 'Notice that I don't mention the word love. I think I've become a little cynical about that, Annis, I'm not even sure that I believe in it any more.' Her ear caught the bitterness in his voice and she wondered what had happened to put it there: a girl who'd rejected him? Someone he couldn't have? Someone who'd died? She was sure that he would never tell her, and she wanted to know . . .

'I need a wife, someone to make a home, someone to come back to, someone to entertain my friends, someone I can talk to. You happen to fit the bill.'

Surely no girl had ever had such a cold-blooded proposal? She said roundly: 'I've never heard such nonsense! There's only one good reason for getting married to someone, and that's because you love them.' She went scarlet then because she had that reason, didn't she, but Jake apparently did not.

'I hope to prove you wrong, darling. Suppose we give it a try? Six months if you like. See how we get on, getting to know each other, becoming friends, nothing more if you don't want that.' He gave her a long austere look. 'That's a promise, Annis.' And when she didn't answer him: 'That's why I'm taking you home tomorrow, so that you can have time to think about it.' He tucked a hand under her arm and began to walk on. 'And don't say no without considering first. You're a sensible girl, and practical, and your head isn't cluttered up with romantic ideas.'

It was on the tip of her tongue to tell him how mistaken he was but that would never do. She said rather primly: 'Very well, I'll think about it.'

'Good. If we go down this path there's a nice little herb garden at its end. Mother started it when she was first married and it's her pride and joy.'

'Oh, is it?' answered Annis blankly: apparently they weren't to mention the subject of their future again.

And indeed, she was right. The rest of the day was spent in the company of Jake's parents. They had tea together and then she was taken upstairs to say goodbye to his grandmother, who lifted a cheek for her to kiss while at the same time observing that she hoped the wedding would be a quiet one, since she couldn't abide too much fuss at her age. Apparently here was the one person sure of their future. The thought was followed by another one: old Mrs Royle wasn't the only one, Annis herself was quite sure, even without pondering the matter too deeply, that she would marry Jake because she loved him, that he was arrogant and far too self-assured and wrapped up in a successful business were things she would have to live with. And she could see no reason why she couldn't make him love her, given time. He had mentioned six months to see how it all worked out, if she couldn't get him interested, to say the least, in that time, then she would have to think again. She bade his parents goodbye with composure and got into the car beside him, answering his small talk on their way to Bath with an equal composure.

They had dinner together later and over it Jake began to tell her something of his work. He was highly successful, but he didn't stress the fact, merely mentioning that he had to travel a good deal. 'You like flying?' he asked her casually.

'I've never been in a plane.' Probably, thought Annis, she was the only girl in the country who hadn't. She added by way of an explanation: 'There are too many of us, you see. The children have heaps of friends and go away in their school holidays, but we don't all go away together.'

She started to work out what a holiday—say, in Italy—would cost if the eight of them went for two weeks and her mind boggled.

'Just so,' observed Jake, watching her face with amusement. 'But you live in a beautiful part of the country, don't you?'

'Oh, yes, and there's always such a lot to do . . .' A look of unease came over her face. She had remembered that if she married Jake there would be no one to help her father. Mary wasn't home and it

wasn't likely that she would be, and Emma was
barely twelve and her mother had far too much to
do around the house. She lifted a troubled face to
his. 'I'd forgotten,' she said simply, and didn't have
to go on because he had understood at once.

'Naturally if you were to—er—leave home, I would
take steps to see that there was someone to fill your
shoes. That's a small matter, Annis, easily dealt with.'

The way he said it, she actually believed him.

They left the next morning in pouring rain and
were back at the Rectory in plenty of time for lunch.
Annis hadn't telephoned her mother, and the look
on that lady's face as they went indoors told her at
once that lunch was to have been a scrappy affair
with no one there but her parents. Annis left the
men in her father's study and repaired to the kitchen.
She had her final week's salary in her pocket, and
though she hadn't earned nearly as much as she had
hoped, there was enough to fill the larder at least.
With their heads together, she and her mother concocted a decent meal and she left her parent peeling
potatoes while she flew down to the village shop,
coming back presently with a laden basket, and
viewed with some interest by Jake from the study
window.

The Rector, joining him at the window, observed
gently: 'I see Annis has been down to the village.'
He added hopefully: 'We ought to get a splendid
lunch.'

Jake turned to look at him. 'I should like to marry
your daughter, sir.'

The Rector took off his glasses, polished them and
put them on again—the better, presumably, to look
at Jake.

'She will make a splendid wife,' he observed. 'As long as that's what she wishes to do, I've no objection and I'm sure her mother won't have any.' He chuckled. 'We have four daughters, you know, and mothers like daughters to get married.'

'Annis is concerned about the amount of work she'll leave you with . . .'

'True, very true, but difficulties are made to be overcome.'

'And if you'll allow me, this is one difficulty which can be overcome easily enough.'

'You're a clever young man, doubtless you know the answer. I really feel that we might have a glass of sherry . . .'

'Annis hasn't agreed to marry me yet.' Jake's voice held amusement.

'No? She never was a girl to be hurried. Give her time.'

'I intend to. I should like, if I may, to come and see her in a few days' time.'

'Of course, we shall be delighted to put you up. You intend to remain in England for the time being?'

'Yes—I may have to go abroad for a few days from time to time, Annis would naturally go with me if she wanted to.'

The Rector chuckled, 'She'll be a fool if she doesn't. She's hardly ever been out of the country, you know.'

Annis, going along the short stone passage leading to her father's study, heard them laughing together. She looked rather less than her usual neat self; there had been a lot to do in the kitchen, but now a nicely cooked meal was ready and she thanked heaven that the men had found each other's company pleasant and not noticed the time. She opened the door. 'Sorry we weren't quite ready for you,' she told them, 'but everything's on the table now.'

No one mentioned getting married over their meal, although Mrs Fothergill, interpreting her husband's speaking look more or less accurately, was bursting to ask questions. The conversation was strictly general, and it wasn't until Annis was in the kitchen again with her mother that that lady was able to indulge her curiosity.

'Tell me about Jake,' she demanded. 'There is something, isn't there?'

'Not yet, Mother. He's asked me to marry him, but I haven't said I will.'

'You're going to? You love him?' And when Annis nodded, 'That's all that counts, my dear. I couldn't wish for anyone better for you—only do remember you've got red hair,' she added obscurely.

Annis stacked the dishes tidily and turned on the tap. 'I don't know anything much about this man,' she volunteered.

Her mother wasn't listening. 'A quiet wedding,' she murmured. 'We can have the reception here. Phyllis Avery will be as mad as fire, she always wanted you for Matt.'

Annis was washing up briskly. 'Matt's keen on Mary.'

Mrs Fothergill brightened. 'Oh, I wondered . . . that would do just as well, wouldn't it?'

'Much better,' Annis assured her. 'Do you suppose Jake will stay for tea?'

He stayed for tea and for supper too, eating macaroni cheese and drinking cocoa as though they were his favourite diet, and when finally he went, his leavetaking was so friendly that Mrs Fothergill, watching the tail lights of his car disappearing down the lane, remarked: 'What a dear boy he is. I'm sorry to see him go.'

Annis silently agreed with her. Jake had bidden her a pleasant, rather casual goodbye with the half promise that he would be back in three or four days. It was only as he was leaving that he mentioned that he would be flying to Brussels in the morning. Mrs Fothergill, to whom a day trip to Bath was a major event, was impressed.

Annis, anxious not to be caught up in her mother's cross-questioning, saw Audrey off to bed, made sure that Emma would follow her and came down again to help James with his maths. And by the time they had washed the supper things, she was able to go to bed herself.

'We could have a little talk,' said her mother hopefully.

Annis kissed her fondly. 'And so we will, darling— tomorrow. I'm a bit tired, and you must be too.'

The next morning, as they made the beds together, Mrs Fothergill asked anxiously: 'You're going to marry Jake, aren't you, dear?'

Annis said slowly: 'I think that perhaps I love him more than he does me.' She sighed. 'Does that matter?'

Mrs Fothergill frowned. 'Darling, I don't see how you can be sure—I mean that Jake doesn't love you as much as you love him, he's not the kind of man to wear his heart on his sleeves, is he? I think in your shoes I'd take the risk.' She added softly: 'Love is very strong, darling.'

Annis took herself off for a long walk that afternoon, the same walk she had taken with her brothers and sisters not so many weeks ago. There was spring in the air now and the going was easier. She paused when she reached the spot where she had first met Jake and tried to remember what she had thought then, but that was obscured by her love now. All she could think was that she loved him very much and life wouldn't be the same ever again if she were to let him go out of her life.

Jake came again three days later after telephoning from the airport, so that they had time to add soup to the supper menu and Mrs Fothergill was able to make one of her mouthwatering pies. And the Reverend Mr Fothergill, shaken from his habitual calm, fetched two bottles of claret from the cellar; the last two there, as it happened.

But if Annis had expected a romantic reunion, she was doomed to disappointment. Jake took her hand briefly, dropped a kiss on her cheek and turned to her mother and father. 'Not inconvenient, I hope?' he wanted to know. 'I have to go to Washington in a week's time.'

They had tea round the fire and James, Emma and little Audrey did most of the talking, but presently when the tea things had been cleared, Jake said: 'Does anyone mind if Annis and I go somewhere and talk for a while?' He glanced out of the window. 'It nice enough to go for a walk.'

She got to her feet. 'I'll fetch a coat,' she said quietly, and when she got downstairs again, he was waiting in the hall for her.

They walked in almost complete silence until they reached the spot where they had first met. 'This seems an appropriate place,' observed Jake cheerfully. 'Are you going to marry me, Annis?'

She looked away from him to hide the disappointment in her face. He was being so matter-of-fact, so businesslike—but then wasn't their marriage going to be that too? At least for the first few months . . .

She said in a clear voice: 'Yes, Jake, I'll marry you—on—on the conditions you mentioned. 'I don't know much about you, I can't even begin to—well, I have to get used to you . . .'

'You'll have every opportunity. I'm going to be rather busy for a month or so, but whenever I have to travel you shall come with me, and if you're interested I shall tell you something of my work. I suggest that we get married quite soon. I have to go to Lisbon at the end of the month, we might get married in time to go there together. I hope you share Grandmother's views about big weddings.'

Annis had no doubt in her mind that his granny had had a wonderful and very grand wedding—white satin, orange blossom, bridesmaids, the lot. It seemed that she herself was going to have to make do with a two-piece and a hat . . .!

'You'll wear white, of course.' Jake's voice broke into her musings. 'Girls like wedding veils and so on, don't they, and I wouldn't want to deprive you, but could we keep the numbers down—family and close friends?'

'Yes. Father and Mother couldn't afford a big reception anyway, and I'd like it to be at home.'

'Good. Let me know as soon as you've laid your plans—about three weeks' time? Don't bother with clothes, you can get all you want later.' He added: 'I'm a rich man, Annis.'

'Yes, I thought you might be, that's why I'm not absolutely certain . . .'

'That's silly of you. Money makes no difference at all, not the way you're looking at it, at any rate—besides, as I said before, you've got too much good sense.' He bent and kissed her suddenly and she drew back quickly before she could fling her arms round his neck.

'That's by way of being a betrothal kiss,' he said, and his voice was dry. 'I won't make a habit of it'.

They began to walk on. 'I'd like you to come up to town tomorrow and see my flat—your people won't mind if we get back late?'

'No, of course not. I—we'd better tell them; Mother will want to invite people and plan the food . . .'

'I'll come over for you all one day next week, and your parents can meet mine. In the meantime they can send the invitations out and so on. Not more than fifty on each side, would you say?'

Annis nodded, outwardly as cool and casual as he, while her insides quivered with excitement and her mind raced. A Vogue pattern for her dress—she would have to make it herself with her mother's help—and they could manage food for the reception between them. Audrey and Emma would be bridesmaids—Laura Ashley print wasn't too expensive, and she could make their dresses too . . . She was quite absorbed, and Jake, looking down at her, smiled a little. She looked quite beautiful in her old coat, her vivid hair blowing in all directions. She would pay for dressing, he could see her in his mind's eye at the foot of his table, entertaining his guests, running his house without fuss, listening intelli-

gently to what he had to say. He had had his fair
share of girl-friends, but he had never until now felt
the urge to marry, and he wasn't quite sure why he
wanted to do so now. Perhaps he was tired of a
bachelor existence, certainly he had wished during
the last few months that there had been someone to
welcome him at the end of a day's work. But he
hadn't wanted a romantic attachment; it was a long
while ago since he had come to grief there. He said
thoughtfully: 'Grandmother will be delighted,' and
Annis thought sadly that it would have been nice if
he had said just once that he was delighted too, but
he didn't add anything, and presently she said: 'She's
a very nice old lady, and I like your parents.'

They walked a long way making a few vague
plans, but she sensed that Jake wasn't really interested in those. She began to ask him questions about
the work he did and for the rest of the walk he talked
about that. A busy life, she gathered, but in between
whiles, a social one too; she rather dreaded that part
of it.

CHAPTER FIVE

THEY left after breakfast the next morning, and since Jake had little to say for himself, Annis contented herself with mulling over the previous evening. There had been no doubt at all that her parents were delighted at their news, and the children had been beside themselves with excitement. The wedding plans had been discussed until late, and although she had peeped at Jake once or twice to see if he were bored, he had shown no sign of that, but had joined in with everyone else, suggesting some scheme quietly, agreeing with almost everything. He had been firm about the date, though, when Mrs Fothergill wanted to postpone the wedding for another week, declaring that three weeks wasn't long enough. He had persuaded her with a silkiness which Annis could not but admire; no wonder he was chairman of so many boards! By the end of the evening he had everyone doing exactly as he suggested and nothing but admiring eyes turned in his direction, and that included Hairy and Sapphro. It occurred to her that she knew very little about him, in fact, the more she saw of him the more remote he seemed—about himself, that was. She would have to remedy that smartly.

'You said you lived near Grosvenor Square . . .'

Jake slid past a slow moving Austin using the crown of the road. 'Between it and Green Street, you know where that is?'

She shook her head. 'We always go to Oxford Street and Regent Street if we go to London—shopping, you know.'

'It's quite near Oxford Street. The flat is in a converted house in a narrow side street, nearer the square than Oxford Street. It's remarkably quiet too. I hope you won't find it too different from Millbury. There's no garden, but there's a wide balcony at the back and Green Park and Hyde Park aren't far away.'

'Is it big, the flat?'

'Oh, there's ample room for the two of us. There's a daily housekeeper—Mrs Turner; she sleeps in whenever I want her and when ever I'm away.'

He slowed the car as they approached Egham. 'Shall we stop for coffee? There's quite a good place here.'

It seemed that he didn't want to talk any more about the flat, indeed he brushed aside the one or two tentative questions Annis put and instead told her a little of the places he had been to, and presently, as they neared London he lapsed into silence.

Annis didn't know London well; after a while she became hopelessly lost and she let out a small sigh of relief as Jake stopped the car half way down a short, quiet street lined with terraces of Regency houses, their doors opening on to a short flight of steps to the pavement.

He opened the outside door with his key and ushered her into a small vestibule which in turn opened into a roomy hall. There was a lift there as well as a broad staircase and a porter sitting behind a small desk. Jake nodded to him and made for the stairs, his arm on Annis's.

'A little exercise won't hurt us after the car,' he commented, 'it's not far.' His own front door was the only one on the second floor and he unlocked it briskly. 'Your future home, Annis—our future home, and welcome.'

She strained her ears for a small hint of feeling in his voice, but it sounded disappointingly casual and matter-of-fact. As she was led into the sitting-room she wondered if she was making a dreadful mistake in marrying him, and then, seeing him standing there, large and assured and smiling gently, she knew that she hadn't. She might have bitten off something more than she could chew, but she had strong teeth!

'Why do you look like that?' Jake wanted to know, and looked amused. 'As though you were arming yourself for battle.'

She smiled at him then. 'I didn't imagine it would be like this,' she said the first thing that came into her head. 'It's lovely!'

As indeed it was. The room was a fair size, furnished in pale colours which made a perfect background for the pictures on its walls, landscapes mostly. Annis, who knew very little about such things, thought they were good. She went closer to inspect them. 'That looks like a Turner,' she said thoughtfully.

'It is. Come and see the dining-room.'

This was a smaller room, furnished with an oval Sheraton table and chairs and a delicate sideboard, no pictures on the walls here, but a charming silk wallpaper, a far cry from the faded greens and brown of the Rectory.

They went through another door to the kitchen and Jake said: 'Mrs Turner will be out shopping. I told her not to bother with lunch, we can go out for that, but she'll have tea for us before we go back.'

They went out of the kitchen into the hall again and he turned a corner into a short passage with several doors. 'Bedrooms,' he said briefly. 'I daresay you'll like to have the end one with the balcony. Mine's at this end and there are a couple of bathrooms. Have a look round if you like, there are one or two phone calls I must make.' He nodded over one shoulder. 'I've a small study.'

Left alone, Annis opened a door and looked in. This would be Jake's room—no flowers, dark masculine colours, an austere bedspread but more lovely pictures on the walls. The next door led to a bathroom and the next to a smaller room, very prettily furnished but having an air of not being used very much, there was a bathroom there too, and she admired its comfort before opening the last door. Her room, Jake had said.

It was larger than the others, and lighter, because the french windows opened on to a balcony, wrought iron and roofed with glass. The room was charming, its cream walls toning with the cream and rose brocade curtains and bedspread, its furniture a pale wood she thought might be apple, inlaid with yew. The bedhead was beautifully carved with flowers and wreaths as was the mirror standing on a long table serving as a dressing table. The pictures here were flower paintings and small delicate watercolours of little animals and beside the burnished steel fireplace were two comfortable chairs. A delightful room and one in which she knew she would feel instantly at home. She peered into the adjoining bathroom and wondered who had matched the towels and soaps and jars with such care. Jake hadn't struck her as being the kind of man to bother over-much about such things, but perhaps it was a side of him she hadn't encountered yet.

She sat down at the dressing table and tidied her hair and powdered her nose, then went slowly out of the room. She could hear Jake's voice from behind a closed door as she went down the passage, back to the sitting-room, to sit quietly until he joined her presently.

'Had a good look round?' he wanted to know. 'If you don't like anything, say so and we'll have it altered.'

'It's all perfect,' she told him seriously. 'Did you plan it all yourself?'

The little mocking smile she hated curled his mouth. 'Fishing, darling? Am I to feel flattered, though I can hardly expect jealousy—that's for those in love, isn't it? Just female curiosity? I did most of it myself, but the odd feminine touch was added by whichever girl-friend happened to be here taking an interest.' He added in quite a different voice: 'You needn't mind, Annis, none of them mattered.'

'I wasn't meaning to pry—I'm not very interested in your past life.' And that was a lie if ever there was one, and she a parson's daughter! 'That doesn't mean to say that I'm not interested in you and I expect when we've been married for a while I might ask you things, but that doesn't mean that you have to tell me—but if I do it will only be because I'm curious about something or other.'

Jake was leaning against the table looking at her

and the nasty little smile had gone. 'You're a very nice girl,' he said deliberately. 'I count myself a lucky man to be going to marry you and once we get to know each other, who knows . . .?' And at her look: 'I loved a girl once, Annis, a long time ago now. I've forgotten my love, but not the promise I made myself that I'd never get deeply involved with a girl again. I'm not going to get deeply involved with you, you know that already, and that suits both of us, doesn't it? There's something very restful about you, darling, like an old friend who's ready to listen or laugh at will—and you've a good brain. If I want to talk business I'll be able to without boring you to tears.'

She supposed that this was the highest praise he could give her and with it she would have to be content, for the time being at least. But she would break down the wall he had built around himself, although it would take time. In the meantime she would be what he wanted, a friend ready to laugh or listen—and she would learn to be a good wife. Only she wished he wouldn't call her darling, a word which should mean so much and which meant nothing.

'Thank you for telling me,' she said quietly, 'about the girl, I mean. I'm sorry. That's why you work so hard, I expect, and I hope you will tell me about your business deals when you want to, it's all new to me, and fascinating.'

'It's certainly that; it's a challenge too!' Jake stood up. 'How about lunch? I booked a table for half past one; we can just make it.'

He ushered her into the magnificence of Claridges with the air of a man who had been there before

and took it all rather for granted, and she wasn't
sure if she should be pleased or vexed that he also
took it for granted that she shouldn't be overawed.
Which she was. The thick carpeting, the buzz of
conversation absorbed by the size of the place, the
pink and blue and gold and ivory everywhere; the
elegant women, the executive types escorting them,
the eye-catching staircase, they all combined to make
her aware of her last year's suit, her no longer new
leather handbag and her shoes, brilliantly polished
but as elderly as the handbag. All the same, she sat
down composedly and drank the sherry Jake ordered
for her, then followed the waiter to their table in the
adjoining restaurant. She held her head high, pretending to herself that she was accustomed to strolling into Claridges for lunch any day of the week
which suited her, and strongly under the impression
that the eyes watching her were scorning her suit. As
a matter of fact, they were on her fiery head and
lovely face—appreciative or envious according to
sex.

With discreet help from Jake she chose lobster
patties, tournedos Rossini, pommes de terre Berny,
and when the sweet trolley came, a delicious confec-
tion of ice cream, honey, pear and fudge, helped
nicely on their way by champagne followed by a
bottle of Château Talbot, which she recognised quite
rightly as a claret while remaining unaware of its
price. She took an appreciative sip and pronounced
it very nice, and Jake agreed with her, his eyes
snapping with amusement.

He was entertaining, telling her amusing little
stories of his travels, his work, the deals he had pulled
off, but he made no effort to resume their conversa-

tion in the flat. That, Annis guessed, was to be decently forgotten, perhaps one day he would tell her about the girl he had loved and why he hadn't married her—but that would be a long way ahead, once they had got to know each other and established a sound friendship. Unless of course it didn't work out and they agreed to part. And if ever that happened, she vowed silently, he would never know her real feelings; she'd die first.

'Coffee?' asked Jake gently, and looked at her enquiringly. 'You were very far away just then, darling?'

Annis rushed into speech; a jumble of thanks for her lunch, the heavenly food, and because she had had too much claret, her near-panic at being there at all.

'You're doing very nicely,' he assured her. 'It's time you realised that you're a beautiful young woman, quite able to hold your own wherever you are. You'll be stunning when we've got you some new clothes.'

He had spoken deliberately, his dark eyes on her face. 'And don't get on your high horse, Annis, you know as well as I do that you'll knock 'em cold in the latest fashion. If you can look beautiful in that blue velvet sack you wore to the Averys' dinner party, you'll attract all eyes in couture.'

She felt rage boiling up inside her, and then suddenly giggled. 'But it was all I had, you know there's never been much opportunity . . .'

'So I gather. I hope you gave it to the church bazaar or sent it to the jumble.'

'As a matter of fact, I gave it to our Mrs Wells; she wanted some new cushion covers.'

Jake let out a bellow of laughter so that people around them turned to look at them, and Annis exclaimed: 'Oh, hush, do, everyone's looking!'

'My dear girl, they've been looking at you ever since we sat down.' He passed his cup for more coffee. 'Shall we go and buy you some dresses now?'

She said no quite firmly, although she couldn't quite keep the regret out of her voice or her face.

'We are engaged, you know,' he said with faint mockery. 'It would be quite proper.'

'Yes, I know . . . it's hard to explain . . .'

He said with a trace of impatience: 'Then don't. But I hope you're not going to shy away from a ring?' He looked at her capable, well kept hands clasped before her on the table. 'Have you any preference?'

Her eyes glowed. 'Sapphires—well, a sapphire,' she amended hastily. 'That's if you don't mind.'

He smiled. 'I like them myself. Shall we go and get it now? There's plenty of time before tea.'

They went to Asprey's where a velvet cushion was laid on a table and a selection of rings were laid upon it for her choice. She sat staring down at them; they all looked very expensive, but she had no idea of the price. She looked rather shyly at Jake and when the nice elderly man serving them had moved away for a moment, whispered: 'Jake, they all look very pricey.'

He only smiled at her. 'You'll only be engaged once, darling, so we might as well do the thing properly.'

Which somehow made it all seem very mundane—besides, she sensed that he wasn't very interested; she was to please herself and she had no doubt that he would pay what it cost with the utmost good humour.

She decided on three sapphires, set close together and ringed by diamonds set in gold. It was a beautiful ring, but she took care not to rhapsodise over it, slipping it on to her finger quickly because he was already getting out his cheque book and had shown no sign of wanting to put it on for her. It looked strange there and far too opulent for the rest of her, but it stood for something too, her love, she would be reminded of that each time she looked at it.

They went back to the flat for tea after that, and while Mrs Turner was getting it, Annis thanked Jake with careful warm friendliness. 'It's quite beautiful,' she told him, 'and thank you for being so generous.'

He glanced at her hand. 'It becomes you very well, you made a good choice. We should have bought a wedding ring at the same time. They'll have your size, of course. Have you any preference?'

She wanted to tell him that she wanted most strongly to choose her own wedding ring, but she managed not to. 'No,' she said quietly, 'gold—plain gold. Will you have one too?'

He looked surprised. 'I hadn't given it a thought. But if you want me to I'll get myself one at the same time.'

He sounded as if he was going to buy an extra packet of something on the grocery list, but at least he was willing to wear a ring. Somehow she felt it was a small triumph.

They ate their tea unhurriedly and left immediately after. 'We'll eat on the way,' Jake told her. 'I told your mother not to keep anything hot.' And in the car as they were roaring down the motorway: 'I'll have to leave tomorrow; I've got a board meeting I must attend and if we're going away after the wedding I'd better hurry things forward a bit.'

'When will you be back? There's the time of the wedding to settle and who's to be asked . . .'

'Oh, morning, don't you think? You decide that—and as few guests as possible, don't you agree? Could we whittle them down to about twenty-five on either side? I'll remember to phone Mother about it. I'll come down as soon as I can—at the moment I don't know when that will be.'

And with that Annis had to be content. They stopped in Shaftesbury for dinner and got to the Rectory about ten o'clock, to find her mother and father still up, obviously waiting for them.

The next hour was spent drinking tea, admiring the ring and discussing the wedding, and even if, as Annis suspected, Jake wasn't deeply interested in the conversation, he concealed it very well, agreeing to the plans her mother was making, agreeing too to her father's suggestion about the actual service, apologising with charm because he would have to leave early in the morning. And when they went up to bed, he kissed her lightly on her cheek in a fashion which won her mother's approval: Mrs Fothergill, while romantic at heart, deplored demonstrative affection before an audience. 'You'll see each other in the morning,' she observed comfortably as she followed Annis upstairs.

But only briefly. Annis, setting the breakfast she had cooked for him on the table, hoped in vain for a word or two of regret at his having to leave her. Beyond thanking her for her efforts, he ate the meal in silence, his mind, she had no doubt, already on his forthcoming board meeting.

Beyond a hasty peck on her cheek and a terse: 'I'll ring you,' he had nothing further to say. She stood at the door, watching the car out of sight, feeling lost.

Her mother came down presently. 'I waited until Jake had gone,' she said. 'I knew you'd want to be together.' She sighed and smiled. 'You aren't going to see much of each other before the wedding, are you?'

'No, but everything's decided, isn't it? We can go ahead with the invitations and we'd better go to Bath and get the material for my dress and the little girls.' Annis smiled brightly at her mother. 'We're going to be busy, darling.'

Which they were. Mrs Fothergill hadn't enjoyed herself so much in years, she confided to Annis, even though money was tight. And Annis, her mouth full of pins, cutting out her wedding dress on the drawing-room floor, had to agree with her; the house rang with excited voices and the kitchen table was littered with lists of food and drink, recipes for canapés and replies to invitations. Annis was to be forgiven if she rather lost sight of Jake for a week or two. True, he had phoned from time to time, but she knew that he didn't want to be bothered with details; as long as she was there, walking down the aisle on Colonel Avery's arm on the stroke of half past ten, nothing else mattered very much.

It was Matt who was her right hand—taking the dog for a walk if she hadn't the time, driving up to Bath to collect the material she had ordered, driving her to Salisbury to get her slippers, sitting at the kitchen table, laboriously stoning fruit for the cake, which Mrs Fothergill had decided to make herself. Annis and she were both clever cooks; they could ice it together and no one would know.

Mr and Mrs Royle came over one day, bringing with them a dozen bottles of champagne which they declared they had been saving for their son's wedding, and the two ladies, luckily taking to each other on sight, spent a delightful afternoon mulling over their own weddings and this one in particular. 'Such a beautiful girl,' sighed Mrs Royle, 'and so sweet, and a good housewife, I'm sure—not that she'll have to bother overmuch with that. Jake has an excellent housekeeper. The house we live in will be his one day, of course, but I believe he's thinking of buying one for himself. There's a delightful place going at Gilford St Charles, and of course Aunt Dora's house in Bath is his now.'

Mrs Fothergill's bosom swelled with pride; her dear Annis had done well for herself. Jake was a splendid man, good-looking, comfortably off, clever—and Annis loved him. He loved her, of course, otherwise he wouldn't have asked her to marry him. 'They'll make a splendid couple,' she observed proudly, and her companion agreed.

There was only a week to go when Jake arrived early one afternoon. Annis was grooming Nancy, escaping for an hour from white satin, bridesmaids' dresses and whether or not the potted plants Mrs Avery had sent over would be too large for the drawing-room. She was in slacks, wellingtons and an old shirt of Edward's and her hair was tied back in a no-nonsense fashion which on any other girl would have rendered her plain.

'I just hope,' said Annis to the donkey as she started on her shaggy coat, 'that they remember to look after you properly—there's your hoofs to be done in May, and the vet had better have another look at those teeth . . .'

'I see no reason why we shouldn't be able to pay a visit before then,' observed Jake from the door. He startled her so much that she dropped the brush and spun round to face him, her mouth open, her eyes surprised.

'My goodness, you gave me a fright!' and when he walked over and kissed the top of her tousled head: 'How nice to see you.' And then, fearful of not appearing sufficiently pleased at his arrival: 'Are you staying?'

'For the night, if I may. I must go home on the way back,' he added dryly. 'I'll be back in time for the wedding. Is everything fixed up?'

Annis had picked up the brush and was working away at Nancy's coat: it gave her something to do. She was feeling strangely shy. 'If I'd known I'd have tidied myself . . .'

Jake was lounging against the side of the stall. 'You look charming as you are. Have you nearly finished, or shall I give you a hand?'

She looked at the impeccable grey suit, the silk shirt and the Italian silk tie. 'I've nearly finished,' she told him, and suited the action to the word, rewarding Nancy with a carrot and bidding her to be a good girl.

'Have you been busy?' she asked as they walked towards the house.

'Very. I should warn you that I shall have to meet one or two people while we're away. I hope we shall be able to get away for a week or so during the summer.'

'We'll be at the flat?'

He shot her a quick glance. 'Yes—at least you will, I may be travelling from time to time. You can come here as often as you like. I've ordered a car for you so that you can get about—a small Talbot . . .'

Annis stopped in her tracks. 'Jake—oh, Jake, how absolutely super! Just for me?'

'Just for you. It will make you independent—you can go wherever you want, within reason.'

She was silent. She didn't want to be independent and if she went anywhere she wanted to be with him, but quite obviously he didn't feel the same way. 'Thank you very much, Jake, it's very kind of you, and thoughtful. I shall love driving it and I'll be able to come home if—if you're away.'

'That's what I thought; no need for you to moon around on your own at the flat.'

It sounded bleak put like that, but she refused to be daunted. She said cheerfully: 'No, of course not. Does Mother know you're here? We'll have supper early if you like.'

Jake was gone the next morning with a parting: 'Shan't be able to get down until the wedding, I'm afraid, so I'll see you at the church.'

Her face was serene as she waved him goodbye, but back in her room she allowed herself the luxury of a good cry, knowing that if her mother noticed her red eyes—and she would, of course—she would put it down to a quite natural reluctance to say goodbye to Jake.

The few days left went quickly with the house in a ferment of cleaning and polishing, china, stored for years top shelves of deep Victorian cupboards, brought out to be washed and stacked neatly, cutlery to be polished, glasses to be burnished, the menu conned again and again and everything needed for it. There was the cake to admire too, looking positively professional after Annis and her mother had spent back-aching hours icing it. Now there was only the baking to do and the sandwiches to make, and that was last-minute work.

Annis, decorating the church with flowers sent over by Mrs Avery, heaved a sigh of relief that by this time tomorrow it would all be over. If this was a quiet country wedding, what must a big affair be like! But then, of course, there would be caterers and someone to do the flowers and a hairdresser. Which reminded her that she would have to wash her hair when she got home.

Matt came into the church just as she was gathering up the mess she had made. 'That looks nice,' he told her. 'Lord, Annis, I never thought when I introduced you to Jake that you'd be getting married within a month or too.

'Nor did I,' said Annis soberly. 'I can't quite believe it, even now.'

'You'll come down and see us?'

'Of course. Jake's given me a car, so when he's away I can drive myself.'

'Won't you go with him?'

'I expect I shall sometimes, but perhaps it won't always be convenient.'

Something in her face stopped him from saying more. 'Everyone's home for the big event, I suppose?'

Annis nodded. 'Yes, Mary got here this morning,

Edward came last night.' She frowned. 'I hope it isn't going to be too much for Mother—I mean, the children . . .'

'I don't see why it should be, they're all at school and there's only little Audrey who needs an eye kept on her, and I'll do that.'

'Oh, will you, Matt? Thanks awfully. She's still so small.'

Matt scuffed his shoe on some ancient brass let into the church floor. 'Well, I'm almost family, aren't I? Besides, I'm going to marry Mary.'

'I thought perhaps you might. I'm so glad. Does she know?'

'Well, in a way. We'll wait until she's finished her training. Mother always thought it would be you.' He took the odds and ends of stalks and leaves from her as they started to leave the church.

'Yes, I know—what a crazy idea!' They laughed together as they went back to the Rectory, where Matt was instantly pressed into moving furniture out of the drawing-room and Annis, much against her will, was told to go upstairs and do something about her hands.

'There's some pale pink varnish on my dressing table,' Mary told her. 'For heaven's sake use it, Annis and rub in lots of cream.'

By the time Annis came down again, her hands nicely done and her hair washed and still damp, the relations had begun to arrive. Not many of them, and there were rooms enough in the Rectory to house them all. Supper was a noisy family party, and directly after it, Emma and Audrey were sent to bed so that they would be up early. Annis was sent to bed too, with strict instructions to stay in bed in the morning. 'Breakfast in bed,' ordered her mother, 'and you'll have to be up and getting dressed directly after.'

So she went obediently up the stairs and into her room. Her case was packed with the new clothes they had somehow contrived to buy: not very many of them, but what there was was good. And her wedding dress hung in the wardrobe, white satin, very simply made, with the plain net veil folded neatly over the shabby chair by the window. The shoes were there too, narrow white satin with little heels because she was a tall girl already and didn't want to tower over Colonel Avery as they went down the aisle. She went and sat down at the mirror and stared at her face. It looked back at her, a little apprehensive as well as excited. She wished she could have seen Jake for just a little while that evening. She was suddenly afraid that perhaps she had bitten off more than she could chew.

'Have I been a fool?' she asked her reflection, and naturally got no answer. Not then, at any rate.

She had it the next morning, going down the aisle on the Colonel's stout arm, a vision of loveliness even if a little pale; her hair blazing above the white satin of her gown, only half hidden by her veil. She looked calm and serene, although her insides were churning with excitement, but her eyes sought Jake's large, reassuring figure the minute they entered the church. He was standing with his back to her, but he turned his head as Mrs Twigg at the organ broke into an enthusiastic rendering of, 'Oh, perfect love,' and smiled. The smile was for Annis alone and she smiled back at him. He might not love her, but she loved him enough for both of them—a dicey state of affairs, she thought dreamily as they paced through the little church, but a challenge. She lifted her chin; she liked a challenge and she had her answer—even if she was a fool, she was a loving fool. Was it John Donne who wrote, 'I am two fools for loving thee . . .?'

She was standing beside Jake now. His hand caught hers for a second and gave it a friendly squeeze and she looked up at him, searching, even at that last minute, for what she longed to see . . . It wasn't there, but in his face there was liking and even affection. They would do to go on with.

CHAPTER SIX

GOING down the aisle, her hand tucked in Jake's, Annis had the sensation that she was in a dream. The church was packed, for not only had the invited guests come, but the village had turned out, man, woman and child. Even old Mrs Crocker in her wheelchair had been parked by the font so that she could get a good view. She smiled and nodded, touched that they had all come to wish them happiness. Mrs Phipps from the village pub had got a new hat—a large felt, wide-brimmed, quite unsuitable for anything but a wedding, but then there were still five of the Rector's children . . . and Phipps himself, with whom she had had many a wordy tussle about sending the children to Sunday School, was beaming at her with all the goodwill in the world. And Mrs Wells wearing one of Mrs Fothergill's old hats, sent to the jumble sale, last year . . . Annis passed them all and then paused with Jake in the porch while the photographer took a picture, to the great delight of the Sunday School class, posed to throw confetti.

'Who said it was to be a quiet wedding?' asked Jake as they drove the short distance to the Rectory.

'Well, I've lived here all my life,' Annis pointed out almost apologetically. 'Besides, it makes a bit of excitement . . .'

She was relieved to hear his laugh.

The reception was, from the villagers' point of view, a resounding success. The some seventy-odd guests Jake and Annis had finally agreed on inviting were swelled, not altogether legitimately, by those living in the village who had the nous to walk through the open Rectory door and join everyone else. Nobody minded, and if the Rector had qualms about the way the champagne was being got through by those who shouldn't be there, he was too good a man to say anything. The sandwiches and vol-au-vents and tiny sausage rolls Annis and her mother had slaved over were gobbled up as fast as they appeared, and it was only because Mrs Fothergill slipped away with some of the wedding cake, to hide it in a tin in the kitchen, that there was any of that saved, either.

What with the speeches and telegrams and everyone wanting to say a few words to the bride and groom, it was a good deal later than they had planned by the time Annis and Jake got into the car, to drive off in another hail of confetti and shouts of, 'Good luck!' from the mass of people on the Rectory lawn, swelled to vast proportions now by the rest of the village who had just popped up to have a quick look.

Out of the village, Jake pulled up, got out and removed the old boot, the coloured balloons and the chalked messages scrawled on the back of the car.

'I suspect the hand of brother James,' he observed as he got back in. 'Be sure to remind me to do the same on his wedding day.'

Which remark gave Annis a pleasant little glow because it sounded so permanent.

'Did you get anything to eat?' he asked her.

'Me? Oh, a sandwich or two and a piece of cake. Why?'

'We shan't have time to stop for dinner—not if we're to catch the plane I've got tickets for. We can have supper in Lisbon.' He made it sound as though Lisbon was just round the corner.

And after that they hardly spoke while the Bentley slid with silent power up the motorway towards Heathrow.

There was someone waiting to take the car when they reached the airport and a porter to take their luggage, and because they had cut it rather fine there was no queueing, just a brisk walk along endless corridors after they had gone through Customs. They were the last on board the plane and since they were travelling first class they had the compartment more or less to themselves. Annis, excited now, strove to look as though she'd done it all before—all the same Jake had to do up her seat belt for her and reassure her as the plane began to move forward. She wasn't exactly nervous, she hastened to assure him, but it was the first time . . .

'It's exactly like a bus without the stops,' he assured her kindly, 'and it's a very short flight.'

It seemed even shorter by reason of the coffee and sandwiches, the drinks, the magazines and papers, interlarded by Jake's casual talk. In no time at all the lights of Lisbon were pointed out to her and they were coming in to land.

There was a car waiting for them at the airport. Annis, accustomed to queue for a bus or wait for a taxi, wondered if this was the way in which Jake always travelled or whether it was because they were on their honeymoon, although perhaps honeymoon wasn't quite the right word; after all, Jake had some business to attend to while they were there. She refused to think about that and looked out of the window at the brightly lighted streets. Presently they crossed an enormous square with a magnificent archway facing the sea, and opening out on to a broad tree-lined avenue.

'The best shops are here,' said Jake, breaking into her thoughts, 'You can get a taxi from the hotel easily enough.'

Annis said, 'Yes, of course,' in a bright voice, wondering if he would be free to spend any time with her at all, and then went on, just as brightly: 'This is a beautiful avenue . . .'

'It stretches for miles; there is a wonderful tropical palm garden at its end. We'll find time to go there. Here is the hotel.'

A magnificent building, streaming with bright lights, exuding luxury from every window. They went inside and someone—the manager, Annis supposed—came to meet them, before handing them over to a porter, who ushered them into a lift and sent them soaring up to the third floor.

Their rooms were at the back—because of the noise, Jake explained—and overlooked a large garden. There was a small sitting-room dividing them and a bathroom at each end, and Annis, never having seen anything like it before in her life, gaped at the marble bath and piles of thick towels.

She wandered back into her room presently, admiring the dark, heavy furniture, the bowl of flowers, the fruit arranged so invitingly on a little table. This was certainly something to tell everyone when she got home again. She pulled herself up short; she would have another home now, with Jake.

The sitting-room was charming and long windows

opened on to a balcony. She went outside and looked around her. It was evening now, at home they would be thinking about going to bed, but from the subdued noise coming from the streets, everyone here was still very much awake. A pang of homesickness made her gulp and she turned away to find Jake standing just behind her, watching her.

'All rather different, isn't it?' he asked. 'And it's been an exciting day for you too. I've asked them to send a meal up here—I think you'll like that better than going down to the restaurant at this time of the evening.'

'Thank you, Jake—it's all rather strange. I expect you've seen it all before and you're used to travelling.'

'Yes, but it's lonely sometimes. I'm not doing anything tomorrow, we'll have a day sightseeing, if you like.' He crossed to a cabinet against a wall. 'We'll have a drink before dinner, shall we?'

And when she was sipping her sherry: 'You'll have plenty to write home about. Little Audrey wanted to come with us, didn't she? We must send her a postcard. You can ring your mother up in the morning, too—it's a bit late now, isn't it?'

Annis looked at him with gratitude. 'I'd love to, and I'm glad you don't have to work tomorrow. I don't know much about Lisbon . . .'

'I'll tell you something about it while we eat. Here's the waiter . . .'

The meal was delicious, although she wasn't sure what she was eating. They drank *vinho verde* with it and then sat for a little while over dark, rich coffee, until Jake said briskly: 'You look like a tawny owl. Go to bed, Annis.'

She wished him goodnight, giving him a quick kiss on the cheek, because all her life she had kissed her parents goodnight and it was going to be a habit hard to break. As she undressed she must remember, she told herself sleepily, not to do it anymore. There was an awful lot to remember if their marriage was to be a success; Jake had suggested six months living together on nothing more than a friendly footing, but she thought they would know long before then if it was going to work out. Of course, she reminded herself, yawning hugely, she already knew her own mind. All she had to do was to make Jake fall in love with her.

She curled up in bed, her wits already woolly with sleep. Was it possible for a man to fall in love with someone he regarded as nothing more than a friend and partner? She wasn't sure, and she was far too tired to bother.

Breakfast was a disappointingly silent meal—not that Jake was ill-tempered, merely that he wasn't accustomed to talking at that meal; he had the *Telegraph* and the *Financial Times* folded by his plate, and after he had asked her if she had slept well, and what she would like to eat, he had nothing more to say. So Annis ate her rolls and ham and fruit and drank the three cups of coffee, not saying anything at all until he finally put the paper down, passing his cup for more coffee as he did so.

'I'm sorry,' he told her, half laughing, 'I'm so used to breakfasting by myself and I do enjoy the peace and quiet.'

Annis's fine eyes flashed with instant rage. If that was how he felt why in heaven's name had he married her? She said with the utmost sweetness: 'I like peace and quiet too, perhaps you could order me a newspaper each morning?'

Jake put down his coffee cup. 'You sound just like a wife,' he observed blandly.

'Well, I am, aren't I?'

'Certainly you are. I'll mend my ways at once, otherwise your hair will catch fire.'

He was laughing at her and after a moment she burst out laughing too. 'I promise I won't nag,' she told him. 'Do you have to work at all today?' She gave him a direct look. 'Because if you want to, that's O.K.—you did say you had to come here on business, you don't have to take me out . . .'

He lounged back in his chair looking at her. 'I've a meeting tomorrow morning, but until then I'm free. I thought we'd take a look at the town: you'd like to see the shops, wouldn't you?' And when she nodded: 'As soon as we get back, I'll arrange for you to have an account at my bank, in the meantime we'll get some *escudos* for you.'

'I've got a little money,' began Annis, conscious of the few pounds in her purse.

'Now you're my wife, I prefer to give you an allowance.' Jake sounded austere, so she took the hint and said no more about it, only went to get the knitted jacket which went with the dress she had bought: a pretty knitted cotton in a pale coffee shade which brought out the best in her hair. It was a warm day and the sky was blue. Crossing the foyer with Jake, she felt suddenly elated. Things would turn out all right. They were already good friends; he liked her. She would have to present a different image in a little while, just enough to startle him out of his acceptance of her as a good friend and nothing

else. She almost skipped out of the door, only remembering just in time that she was now a married
lady and must mind her manners.

There was a car outside, with a man lounging in
the driver's seat, but he got out when they reached
him, said something to Jake and went away.

'I've rented a car,' Jake explained, holding the
door open for her. 'It saves a great deal of time, and
we can get around more.'

He drove down the long avenue, back towards
the square she remembered, but just before they
reached it, he parked the car and invited her to get
out. The street was lined with elegant shops, but he
walked her past the first two or three and opened
the door of a jewellers.

'I haven't bought you a wedding present,' he explained, and she went red, remembering the leather
wallet she had bought for him and then hidden away
in her case because if she had given it to him, he
might have felt compelled to get her something in
return.

Jake eyed her with amusement. 'You should blush
more often,' he told her. 'It suits you.'

'There's no need——' she began, but he wasn't
listening, and already there was a small dark man
advancing to meet them, bowing and smiling.

'Mr Royle,' he bowed again. 'I am delighted that
you come again.'

So he'd been before—buying what for whom?
Annis glanced up at Jake and encountered a look of
such amusement that she felt her cheeks grow hot
again. She heard him say airily: 'You see now why it
is such an advantage to have no—er—sentimental
feelings about each other.' His smile mocked her.

'Earrings, I think. Shall we see if there is something which will match your ring?'

She sat down obediently on a little velvet chair before a small table with a winged mirror, and presently, deep in the enthralling task of trying on one jewel after another, she quite forgot what she had been angry about. They settled on a charming pair; sapphire drops surrounded by diamonds hanging from a short diamond-studded chain. Annis, examining them in the mirror, thought them exquisite. 'I'd like to keep them on,' she decided.

'Why not?' agreed Jake idly, writing a cheque.

They were on their way out when she stopped to admire an antique brooch, a true lovers' knot from which was suspended a little diamond heart.

And when Jake asked: 'Do you like that?' she said quite unthinkingly: 'It's lovely!'

Jake nodded to the salesman. Before she could protest the brooch had been taken from the glass case, encased lovingly in velvet, and Jake was writing another cheque.

'But I didn't mean . . . that is, you had no need to buy it. I've got my present.'

'I've yet to hear a law stating that a man may not give his wife whatever he chooses.' He grinned wickedly at her. 'Let's go and look at some dresses.'

'But I've got three new . . .' she stopped at the look in his eye, and said meekly: 'All right Jake.'

An hour later they were in the car again, the boot cluttered up by a number of dress boxes. They had stopped for coffee at a little pavement café and now they were on their way to the tropical garden. Four dresses, thought Annis happily, and almost choked at the memory of their price. But Jake hadn't turned a hair, indeed he had urged her to buy the ones she had deliberately discarded because they were very expensive. So she had. She sat now, going over their perfections in her mind, not noticing anything much until Jake slowed the car and turned into what appeared to be the beginnings of a park.

There was a small gate to one side, almost hidden by trees and shrubs, and someone was standing there selling tickets. They went through and Annis, for the moment at least, forgot her new clothes and jewellery. There were ferns and tropical plants all round them, the damp air fragrant with them, little riverlets running in and out amongst their roots and steps cut in rocks so that one could wander at will. They spent an hour there, getting vaguely lost from time to time, discovering a cave hidden away with a pool at its centre and benches against its walls so that one might, if one wished, sit and contemplate the water. And there were ducks and waterfowl and swans and fish. Annis peered and stared, nipped up and down steps and sniffed at the strangely exotic flowers and would have stayed for the rest of the day if Jake hadn't reminded her that it was well past noon.

She said at once: 'Oh, I'm sorry, Jake—I got carried away, I've never seen anything like this before. I hope you've not been bored. Have you been before?'

She wished she hadn't asked that, for his face assumed a bland expression and he said shortly: 'Oh, yes, several times.'

And on one of those times something had happened to make him angry—or unhappy. She thought crossly that it was like reading a book and coming to a page which wasn't there.

But they lunched amicably enough and in the afternoon he drove her to Sintra, where they went round the palace with its strange shaped chimney-pots, and then drove back to the coast to visit Caicais and Estoril. They had tea here, at the very English tea-shop, then drove back to Lisbon in time for Annis to change into one of her new dresses—a pale green crêpe-de-chine which transformed her into a quite breathtakingly lovely girl and made a splendid background for the sapphires. 'And I would have worn the brooch,' she explained to Jake, 'but I thought it might be too much of a good thing.'

He agreed, staring rather hard at her. Excitement had given her a colour and she had done her hair in a careless knot which accentuated her pretty neck. 'Is something the matter?' she asked, seeing his look. 'Do tell me. I'm not used to dressing up, you know.'

'There's nothing wrong,' he said slowly, 'and you—you look charming. Shall we go down?'

The evening was an unqualified success. Annis, rather heady by reason of the admiring glances cast at her and the knowledge that her dress was by far the most charming in the room, drank rather too much champagne, which made her even headier, so that when Jake suggested that they might dance, she was more than willing.

'Mind you,' she warned him, 'I'm not much good. There are dances in the village hall at home, of course, but I daresay they're a bit out of date. And when there's been a disco for the youth club I've gone to help with the food and that sort of thing.' She gave him a disarming smile, a bit hazy because of the champagne. 'I'll do my best, though.'

He didn't answer, only smiled a little and whirled her on to the floor. The band was playing an old-fashioned foxtrot and after a moment or two of fright that she might tread on his feet or use the wrong foot herself, she forgot all about it and enjoyed herself. Jake was a good dancer, and for once she had a partner who was taller than herself; it had always been her fate to be partnered by small men: instead of looking over a head she could only see a black tie.

They danced for a long while, only stopping for a drink from time to time, until Jake said: 'I'm sorry to break up a delightful evening, but I have to be at a meeting at half past eight tomorrow.'

Annis looked up at the ornate gilt clock on the wall by their table. 'But it's one o'clock!' she exclaimed in horror. 'My goodness, why didn't you say so before?'

He sounded surprised. 'I was enjoying myself.'

'Me too.' In their sitting room she wished him goodnight, keeping well away in case he might think that she was going to kiss him again. 'Will you be back for lunch?' she wanted to know brightly.

'I doubt it. Will you be all right? Take a taxi down to the shops and see if you can find something pretty for Audrey. You can have lunch up here if you like—it might be a good idea.'

At the door she paused. 'Thank you for a lovely evening,' she said dreamily. 'It really was super.'

She hadn't been looking forward to being on her own, but it wasn't as bad as she'd expected. A taxi was found for her at once and deposited her near the shops, and she blessed Jake's forethought in stuffing a roll of *escudos* in her handbag, because she hadn't given it a thought. She counted the notes quickly, rather taken aback at the amount; there would be more than enough to buy something for her little sister.

But there was plenty of time. She saw some exquisite handkerchiefs, just the thing for Mary, and a set of embroidered table mats which would do for her mother, by the time she had bought them she felt she deserved her coffee and sat down in the same café she and Jake had gone to. A mistake, as it turned out, because several men asked if they might join her. She dismissed them with an unselfconscious dignity which was far more effective than a display of indignation, drank her coffee at leisure, then went on her way.

She found what she wanted for little Audrey finally, a silver chain, as fine as a spider's thread, with a little cross studded with turquoise at its end. She put the little box in her handbag and waved to a passing taxi: it was almost one o'clock and she was hungry. Pleased too that the morning had passed so quickly without Jake. She had just got in and was giving the driver the name of the hotel when another taxi went past, going slowly. Jake was in it, and sitting beside him was a pretty woman, dark and vivacious and smiling. Smiling at Jake. Annis gave a snort of rage and looked out of the other window. She was sure that Jake hadn't seen her; he'd been staring too hard at his companion. At the hotel she bounced out of the cab, tipped the driver at least twice as much as she needed to, and went inside.

The manager came to meet her, looking fatherly. 'Madam will lunch in her sitting-room?' he asked.

Annis's eyes kindled. 'No, thanks. I'll come down to the restaurant.'

She sailed past him and hurried up the magnificent staircase, arriving a little out of breath on the third floor, but all the better for having worked off some of her temper.

It only took a few minutes to tidy herself, then she went back downstairs again in a more leisurely manner and went into the restaurant. She was given a table for two in the window, where the sunshine shone on her brilliant head and made a lovely picture of her, so that several people looked at her and then looked again. She had disposed of iced melon and was about to start on her lobster Cardinal when a dark, merry-faced youngish man crossed the room and stopped beside her.

'Mrs Royle? You will forgive me, but I am an acquaintance of your husband and I am desolated to see you lunching alone. Would you consider that I should join you? I also am alone. Jake does not come, perhaps?'

Annis put down her fork. 'You know Jake, I don't think he mentioned having friends here . . .'

'Roberto Gonzalez. I am in the wine trade, and our paths have frequently crossed.'

Annis held out a hand. 'Annis Royle. Do sit down, Mr Gonzalez, and have your lunch with me.'

'You are kind.' He took the chair the waiter had drawn from the table, and gave his order. 'You do not drink wine?' he asked. 'You will allow me to order a light white wine—our wines are excellent.'

He was a good talker, and Annis, still smarting from Jake's behaviour, was more than ready to be friendly. They were chatting like old friends over their coffee when she glanced up and saw Jake standing just inside the door.

He didn't smile as he walked towards her, indeed there was no expression on his face at all, which was she found a little intimidating, all the same she smiled up at him and said: 'Hullo, Jake. Have you had lunch? I think you know Mr Gonzalez . . .'

Her companion had got to his feet. 'Your wife was lunching alone and I ventured to suggest that we might share a table. How are you, Jake?'

'Very well, thank you. We must meet and have a chat some time, but now you must forgive us, we have an appointment.'

'Of course—and I also must work, alas. Mrs Royle, it has been a great pleasure meeting you, I hope that we may do so again, and very soon.'

Annis held out a hand and gave him a wide smile, then pinkened when he kissed it instead of shaking it as she had expected. All the same, it was rather nice and perhaps Jake would benefit by a little competition.

Alone with him, she asked cheerfully: 'What appointment?' and when he said briefly: 'We will go to our sitting-room, Annis,' she walked ahead of him out of the restaurant and into the lift, looking, she hoped, cool and composed.

The room was pleasantly cool because the shutters had been closed for an hour or more, but she crossed to the window and opened them to let in the bright sunshine before she turned to face Jake.

'I asked you to have lunch here.' He spoke casually.

'Yes, I know you did, but I felt like being with people. Do you mind?'

'I mind very much. I didn't take you for such a fool, Annis. A pretty—a very pretty girl lunching on her own in a restaurant and picking up any Tom, Dick or Harry who chooses to speak to her.'

'Are you jealous?' asked Annis with interest.

He looked surprised. 'Jealous? I? Heavens, no, but I am annoyed that you deliberately went against my wishes.'

Annis sat down, crossed one long leg over the other and studied her elegant high-heeled shoes. 'I didn't pick anyone up, you know—that was a very nasty thing to say, and quite unjustified. Roberto said he was a friend of yours and he was very pleasant. I like him.' She added dreamily: 'I liked having my hand kissed too.'

She had the satisfaction of seeing Jake wince. 'Well, don't expect me to do anything so silly,' he begged her coldly.

'Of course I don't. It wouldn't be nice if you didn't both like it, would it?' She gave him a limpid glance. 'You said we had an appointment?'

'Only to get rid of Gonzalez. I have to go back almost at once.' He left the door where he had been standing and sat down opposite to her. 'I wanted to make sure that you were all right.' He added nastily: 'Obviously you were. What do you intend doing this afternoon?'

'There's a museum I'd like to see, I've forgotten its name, but the girl at the desk told me that it was wonderful.'

'You'll take a taxi, Annis?'

'Yes, Jake.' She looked so meek that he studied her quiet face for a moment frowning.

'I hope to be back about four o'clock, perhaps a little later.'

'Yes, Jake, I'll be back by then.'

He got up and started for the door and she got up too. She was a little shocked at herself, a parson's daughter, feeling so strongly that she must get even with him. 'Just a minute,' she told him, and went up close and picked something off his shoulder. 'A hair,' she said serenely, 'a long black hair. Shall I get a clothes brush? It would never do to go to a board meeting looking—well, untidy.'

He caught her hand in his and burst out laughing. 'So that's it? You vixen! Shall I tell you who she was?' He caught sight of the time. 'No, I can't—I haven't a minute left.' He kissed her suddenly and very hard and slammed through the door, leaving her a prey to mixed feelings. The worst of which was that if she took exception to anything he did when she wasn't there, he could easily guess that her feelings were rather more than friendly. She had been very silly and childish. She went and sat by the open window, all desire to visit museums gone; she was still there when Jake came quietly in two hours later.

'I finished early,' he told her. 'Did you enjoy the museum?'

She had been so deep in thought that she had a faintly bemused look.

'I didn't go.'

'You've had tea?'

She shook her head and he crossed the room and stood looking down at her. 'You're feeling all right? I'll ring for tea, shall I?'

'Yes, please,' and then: 'Jake, before you do, I'm

sorry for all the silly things I said. I didn't mean
them—I mean, I don't really like having my hand
kissed, you know, and—there wasn't anything on
your shoulder, I made it up.' She added, lying with
sincerity: 'I really don't want to know about your
friends—or what you do when I'm not there. It's
entirely your own business and I'm sorry, I really
am.'

Jake pulled her to her feet and stood with his arms
lightly around her.

'Did I ever tell you what a nice girl you were?'
he asked. 'And I shall mind very much if you
don't take some interest in me, you know. And I'm
sorry too, behaving like a tyrant because you
were lunching with someone. You see, I thought that
you might be lonely and I came back prepared to
. . . well, never mind that now.' He tapped her nose
very gently with a finger. 'And the dark-haired
lady—she's the wife of an old friend of mine,
he couldn't attend the board meeting because
he was under the weather, so she brought down
some important papers to be signed; he had to
sign them too, so I went back with her to get it
done.'

His arms felt very comforting around her.
Everything was going to be all right; she had been
stupid, but she wouldn't make the same mistake
again.

'Thank you for telling me,' she smiled up at him.
'Father always says I jump to conclusions—it must
be my red hair.'

He let her go and dropped a careless kiss on her
bright head as he did so. 'Then I must take care to
remember that, mustn't I? Shall we have tea?—I

had *bifes de atum*—that's tunny fish—for lunch, nice but highly flavoured.'

He crossed the room to ring for a waiter. 'Like to go dancing this evening?' he asked, he sounded casually indulgent, like an old friend.

CHAPTER SEVEN

THEY spent all the next day together. There was nothing that couldn't wait until the following morning, Jake told Annis over breakfast, and how would she like to go to Caicais again; they could lunch at one of the delightful fish restaurants close to the beach and go for a brisk walk along the shore.

And it was a lovely day, even better than she had hoped for. They had spent the morning poking round the shops, buying anything that took their fancy, and drunk their coffee at a small cheerfully canopied café. Lunch had been a success too. Annis had eaten *bacalihau pudim*, which sounded very glamorous even though it was dried cod soufflé, and then *bolo de mei*, a rich cake of honey, cinnamon, spices and nuts. She had drunk the white wine Jake had chosen for her and then, at his suggestion, topped off the lot with a glass of Malmsey. Thus sustained, she was quite prepared for the long walk along the beach, although they didn't hurry; it was delightfully warm, so Annis had left her jacket in the car, and presently she had sat down on a convenient rock, taken off her shoes and done the rest of their walk with bare feet, occasionally going down to the water's edge to dabble in the still rather chilly sea.

They had gone back to the car later and driven to Estoril where they had tea at one of the fashionable hotels along the boulevard and then taken the road through Sintra and so back to Lisbon, tired from their wanderings, but not too tired to dance that evening.

Annis had been careful not to ask Jake if he were free on the following day, too, so she was prepared, more or less, when he told her that he would be away for most of the day. 'But I thought we might have Rosa and Emmanuel to dinner in the evening. I'll arrange a table for four and we can dance afterwards.'

She had agreed quickly, wondering if he found her a dull companion. She had no witty conversation and she tended to talk too much about her family. She made a mental resolve not to mention them for several days.

She sat up in bed, long after they had said goodnight, writing home. There was a great deal to write about and without actually saying so, she implied that Jake was with her all the time; she skimmed over that part rather, but writing a lot about her earrings and brooch and the new dresses and then, because her father would be interested, enlarging at length about Sintra and its history. It was after two o'clock when she finally put down her pen and turned out the light. She made herself dwell on the highlights of the day and went to sleep finally, happy because she had spent all of it with Jake.

She was determined not to be lonely the next day. They had breakfasted early because Jake had to be in the city by half past eight, which left a great deal of the day to get through. Annis took a taxi to the museum and did it very thoroughly before going back to the hotel to have lunch; this time in their sitting room. The shops would be closed until three o'clock, so she read the English newspapers and then took another taxi to the shops in the Chiado. She still had a lot of money in her purse. It was nice to buy presents without bothering too much about the price—cufflinks for Edward, a camera for James, a filigree silver bangle for Emma and, since little Audrey already had a present, a beautifully dressed doll in national costume. Which made it unfair for Emma; Annis settled for a hand-knitted sweater, hoping that she would be able to squeeze it into her luggage; she already had all those extra dresses, and while she was about it, she might as well make room for a delightful pair of kid sandals which caught her eye. They were wildly expensive, but they would go with all her new dresses.

A glance at the time sent her hurrying for a taxi. Jake might already be back at the hotel and they had guests for dinner.

He was sitting with his feet up on another chair when she reached their sitting-room, sleeping peacefully. She stood looking at him for a long minute; he was tired. She looked at him with love and then almost jumped out of her skin when he spoke without opening his eyes.

'Have you had a good day?' One eye surveyed her and her parcels. 'Ah, I see you have.'

'Yes, thank you. I'm sorry I'm late, the shops are terrific . . . have you had tea?'

'I waited for you.' Jake got to his feet, not looking in the least tired now and rang for a waiter. 'Rose and Emmanuel won't be here until half past eight, we have plenty of time.' He pulled a chair forward for her and sat down himself. 'What have you bought?'

Annis opened her parcels, quite forgetting that she wasn't going to mention her family again; she chatted happily while they looked at the things she had bought and then had tea until she remembered. She stopped in mid-sentence and sat staring at him.

'Well, go on,' Jake begged her, and looked surprised when she muttered:

'Oh, it was nothing, I've forgotten what it was I was going to say.' She got up slowly. 'I'd better go and dress.'

'Wear that blue thing with the pleats.'

She was pleased because he remembered that she had some new dresses. She nodded happily and wandered off, her head already full of a daydream wherein she appeared in that same dress and Jake was so overcome at the sight of her in it that he fell in love instantly.

It wasn't quite like that. He was standing at the window, looking out at the evening sky when she joined him. He barely glanced at her, but moved away to get her a drink, glancing at his watch as he did so with the remark that they still had half an hour in which she could enjoy it.

It was a superb sherry, but it could just as well have been tap water as far as Annis was concerned. She was aware that she looked very nice: she had done her hair so that the earrings might show to the best advantage. The diamond brooch looked just right pinned on the bodice of the new dress and the sandals were a pure delight, so why couldn't he look at her just once? After all, he had asked her to wear that particular dress.

She did her best, strolling about the room, sitting with one leg swinging over the other so that he couldn't fail to see the sandals, putting up a hand to touch an earring. He noticed none of these, so that presently she sat primly, her feet tucked beneath her chair, well away from the lamps. She had a childish desire to burst into tears, even scream a little so that she might relieve her feelings. As it was, she answered his random remarks in a polite small voice and longed for them to go down to the restaurant.

They had only to wait a few minutes for their guests. Annis, shaking hands with Rosa, discovered that she was as pretty as she had thought, but a good deal older, and as for Emmanuel, he was rather short and dark with bright dark eyes and a charming manner. Annis had been rather dreading the evening, but after a while she began to enjoy herself. Their guests were amusing and witty and spoke excellent English and there was a seemingly endless stream of small talk. And Emmanuel was a good dancer; she was too tall for him, of course, but she forgot that. It was late when they said goodbye and it was Rosa who said, 'You must both come and dine with us before you leave. When will that be, Annis?'

Annis blinked; she had no idea. Jake said smoothly: 'Five days' time, Rosa, and we'd love to, wouldn't we, darling?'

'Good. I'll telephone you.' She kissed Annis's cheek, offered her own for Jake to salute, and waited while Emmanuel kissed Annis. Social kisses—Annis wasn't sure if she would get used to them, but she supposed she'd have to.

Over breakfast the next morning Jake told her that he had no more meetings for three days and suggested that they might go farther afield, perhaps stay the night somewhere. 'We could drive down to the Algarve,' he suggested. 'There is a good hotel at Praia de Rocha, or we could go to the *pousada* at Sagres, visit Cape St Vincent, see Prince Henry's Fort and watch the fishermen.'

'Oh, please, Jake, that sounds absolutely great. When can we go?'

'Now.'

'Now?' she almost squeaked. 'But I haven't packed . . .'

'You'll only need stuff for the night.' He was laughing at her. 'You can have ten minutes.'

'What about you? Shall I . . .'

He interrupted her. 'It will take me less than five minutes. I'll ring the desk.'

'Are we coming back here?'

'Yes, of course—now run along.'

She flung night things into her overnight bag, added make-up haphazardly, poked a gossamer-fine dress into a corner, added the new sandals, snatched up her shoulder bag and declared herself ready. If she looked faintly dishevelled she wasn't aware of it, and Jake, glancing at her, only smiled; she was such a lovely girl it didn't matter at all.

It was a clear sunny morning and the Salazar bridge across the Tagus, high and slender above the water, looked almost fairylike, but once on it they met the incoming traffic from the south and they were soon surrounded by cars and lorries and un-ending noise, but half way across Annis forgot that, staring at the statue of Christ, high on the hills on the farther side and then down to the busy river and the sprawling city below.

'Is this the only road to the south?' she wanted to know.

'No, but it's one of the busiest. It goes as far as Alfambra before it splits. We'll take the road to Vila Debispo and then on to Cape St Vincent and to Sagres. We can go back through Monchique, over the mountains and get to Lisbon from the south-east.'

They stopped for coffee presently at a small wayside café and then went on through ever changing country, sometimes orange and lemon groves, vines and olive trees, sometimes forests of cork trees, winding up steep slopes and then through a dry and arid countryside. As the morning passed, it became warmer, and with Vila Dobispo behind them, they stopped for lunch, eating it out of doors in front of the inn; sardines grilled over a charcoal fire and a salad, crusty rolls and a local wine to wash them down. The country around them was wooded and hilly, with the mountains behind them and the sea not so very far away. 'We'll park the car at the *pousada*,' said Jake, 'and explore if you're not too tired.'

Annis looked at him in astonishment. 'Me, tired? But I've not done a thing for days!'

The sea when they reached it looked delightful with the sun sparkling on it, lapping the distant rocky coastline and the beaches of Sagres. There were small fishing boats being unloaded and people shopping in the main street as they went through the little town to where the *pousada* stood on a hill overlooking the beach. It looked big and a little bare from the outside, but its interior was charming with a large airy set of rooms sparsely but very comfortably furnished with big chairs grouped invitingly

round coffee tables and upstairs their rooms overlooked the sea with wide doors leading on to a balcony. Annis unpacked in no time at all, gave her
hair and face a very perfunctory going over, and
pronounced herself ready to go out. This wasn't like
the hotel at Lisbon at all; for the first time she felt as
though she were really on holiday. She would have
liked to have told Jake, but it might sound ungrateful.

They spent the rest of the day strolling round the
town, having tea in a café by the beach and buying
postcards. And after dinner that evening they
strolled along the beach and since the evening was
chilly, Annis swathed herself in the shawl Jake had
brought for her that afternoon. She was happy, at
least as happy as she could be, she reminded herself,
and Jake seemed quite content to potter around with
her, although she wasn't sure he wouldn't get bored
after a day or two. But it was only going to be a day
or two, anyway.

'Where do we go tomorrow?' she asked.

'Along the coast road to Portimao, up into the
Monchique Mountains and on back to Lisbon, but
first we'll go to Cape St Vincent and take a quick
look at Prince Henry's fort.'

'It sounds wonderful.' She took a deep breath. 'I
suppose we couldn't stay another day here, Jake?'

They were almost at the hotel again and in the
lamplight she saw his quick frown. 'Afraid not,
Annis, I've several more people to meet. Besides,
we're dining with Rosa and Emmanuel.' She didn't
speak, but perhaps he sensed her disappointment,
for he added kindly: 'We'll go back on an evening
plane and spend the day wherever you like.'

'Oh, Jake, I'd love that! Someone was telling me about the museum of coaches, I'd like to see them, and I wondered could we possibly hear a *fado* singer? Colonel Avery was talking about them and told me that they were quite extraordinary.'

They were standing in one of the airy reception rooms, almost empty because most of the residents were still at dinner. 'Why not? I'll see what can be arranged.' He gave her a gentle nod. 'I daresay you're tired. I'll go along to the desk and settle up, it'll save time in the morning. Sleep well.'

The smile he gave her was placidly friendly: she could have been a well-liked aunt or cousin. She found it difficult to smile back.

They breakfasted early and drove the short distance to Cape St Vincent, where they walked round the lighthouse, bought a hand-embroidered tablecloth from one of the stalls in the shadows and then drove back along the towering clifftop to inspect Prince Henry's Fort, but they didn't stop long here. Annis sensed that Jake was impatient under his impassive good humour and declared herself ready to go on again, sitting quietly beside him as they took the coast road to Portimao.

They stopped for coffee at Praia da Rocha and travelled on, to pause and watch the fishing boats leaving the harbour at Portimao, and then, because the morning was almost gone, turning north to the mountains and Montchique. They lunched there at an *estalagem*, the furniture and the rooms so elegant that Annis didn't quite believe Jake when he told her that it was an inn. They ate seafood and drank Lagos wine, and Annis finished her meal with some little tartlets of figs and almonds and honey, very rich and delicious.

It was nine o'clock before they reached the hotel and Jake suggested that Annis might like to have dinner in their sitting room, but she had already decided that he had had enough of her sole company for the time being; she opted for the restaurant and spent half an hour bathing and changing into one of her new dresses. Rather a waste as it turned out, for Jake was immersed in a sheaf of papers and although he got to his feet when she joined him, he barely glanced at her before going quickly down to dinner—a meal they ate with discreet speed because, he told her, he had a good deal of homework to do before his meeting in the morning.

'Thank you for my two lovely days,' she said as they said goodnight. 'I hope they didn't mean you'll have to work extra hard tomorrow.'

He shrugged enormous shoulders. 'They made a nice break, but I won't see much of you tomorrow, nor the following day. I expect you've got some more shopping to do.'

She answered that she had—a lie told brightly and with no sign of the disappointment she felt.

She filled in the days somehow; she had money to spend, time in which to spend it, and the weather was glorious. She told herself these facts repeatedly and presented a bright face to Jake when he returned in the evening, declaring that she was only too glad to sit with a book while he worked at his endless papers. Not that it would always be like that, he assured her; he had a competent secretary at his London office who coped with a good deal of the spadework.

By the end of the second day she found hersel looking forward to their dinner party with Rosa and Emmanuel; it would be fun to chat over drinks and idle over the meal. Besides, Jake was going to take her out the following day; she had hugged the thought to her during the lonely two days.

She had changed and was sitting on the balcony when he came back in the evening. He greeted her briefly, asked her to pour him a drink and went away to shower and change. There was still time to si quietly before they needed to leave and she didn' bother him with questions; it was obvious that he was tired and, for some reason, ill-tempered.

The reason came to light quickly enough 'Something's come up,' he told her. 'I'm afraid I'l have to go to Setubal—there's a canning industry there—the management have asked me if I'm interested in taking up some shares, and it would be fool-ish to go back home without looking into it. It'l mean I'll go early in the morning and probably be away all day. Perhaps you'd pack for me? We car have dinner before we leave.' He added irritably 'I'm sorry, we shan't be able to spend the day together.'

So that was why he was ill-tempered, building up a bad humour against her expected tantrums and disappointment. She had no intention of giving him the satisfaction, though. She kept her voice pleas-antly quiet, although it was a bit of an effort.

'Well, of course it would be quite stupid to go all the way home without going to see these people, and to tell you the truth, I don't mind a bit: I found a small shop in the Baixa where they sell gold and silver filigree work, only I didn't have time to look properly. Now I'll go there tomorrow and choose something for Mother. I'll have lunch out and come back in plenty of time to pack for both of us.' She returned his hard gaze with a placid smile. 'Did you have a successful day?'

His terse, 'Yes', didn't encourage her to pursue the subject, and presently they went down to the car and drove through the city to its outskirts where Rosa and Emmanuel lived in an old house halfway up the hills overlooking the river.

Later that night, lying awake in her bed, Annis went over their evening. It had been a pleasant one; Rosa and Emmanuel were a delightful couple and they had a beautiful home. Annis had looked at photos of their four children, all in their teens. And agreed with Rosa that families were fun. She hadn't looked at Jake as she had spoken, although she was very well aware that he was listening, and because she had wanted to hurt him, she had added clearly: 'Besides, in a family a child learns to give and take. An only child so often just takes, and will stay that way all his life, poor dear.'

Rosa had patted her hand. 'You and Jake will have lovely children, I am sure,' she had said kindly.

It didn't bear thinking about. Annis gave a great sniff, buried her head in her pillows and had a good cry.

She cried for a long time, so that when finally she went to sleep she was tired and overslept. She didn't wake until Jake's voice from the door roused her. 'I'm just off—sorry if I woke you. You'll be all right?'

He was looking at her intently, although there wasn't much to see beyond a great deal of fiery hair.

Annis, aware that very likely her eyes were red-rimmed and her nose the same colour, prudently kept her face tucked well into the pillows.

'Never better,' she told him cheerfully. 'I hope you have a successful day.' She wished he would go away before she burst into tears again. Instead he came right into the room and stood looking down at her.

'I really am sorry about our day together—you're not too disappointed?'

Her voice was nicely muffled by a pillow. 'Heavens, no. I've never enjoyed myself so much, pottering around on my own—it's luxury after five brothers and sisters, you know.'

His voice was dry. 'I wouldn't know, being an only child. Annis, I'll see you about five o'clock.'

He turned on his heel and went out of the room, closing the door quietly behind him. So he had minded about her remark to Rosa. Annis felt suddenly mean; he had been kind and generous to her and she was ungrateful. She promised herself then and there that she would tell him how sorry she was the moment he came back.

She got up presently and, being a practical girl, planned her day over her breakfast. The shop in the Baixa, since she had told Jake she would be going there, and then the coach museum, so that she could tell Emma and little Audrey and James about it, and she must remember to buy some small present for Mrs Turner. If she didn't hurry, she would be able to fill her day nicely.

All the same, the hours dragged. Long before five o'clock she had packed and changed into travelling clothes, and now she was sitting on the balcony for the last time, warm in the sunshine and a little sleepy. But not too sleepy to remember what she had promised herself that morning; when Jake came into the room she got up at once and went to him.

'Hullo, Jake. Did you have a successful day?' and without waiting for him to speak: 'Jake, I'm sorry about what I said to Rosa yesterday evening, about an only child not giving—I don't know what made me say it. It's not true anyway . . .'

He had put down his case and lounged over to the window. 'My dear girl, what makes you think I would worry about a rather silly remark like that?' His voice was smooth and without expression. 'We solitary ones are blessed with a strong sense of our ability to get ahead of everyone else, didn't you know that? I daresay you would call it arrogance.'

He smiled at her, the nasty little smile she had so disliked when they first met. 'I'm going to shower before dinner—and don't waste your pity on me, darling.' He paused at the door to look at her. 'I wonder why you're making such a thing about it?'

He had gone before she could think of an answer to that.

They had an early dinner in the restaurant and Jake carried on a bland conversation which made it impossible for her to do more than answer him in like vein, and after that there was the quick drive to the airport and the flight back. It was late by the time they reached Heathrow, but the car was there, waiting for them, and the roads fairly empty, so they reached the flat without any delays and Annis, going through the door Jake opened, could hardly believe that a few short hours ago she had been sitting in a hotel in Lisbon.

Mrs Turner had left a note. There was a light supper in the fridge, coffee in the percolater, and she would be round the next morning at her usual time. Annis brought in the tray and put it on a small table while Jake opened the pile of letters waiting for him. There were two for her too—one from her mother and one in Matt's handwriting—but she didn't open them at once. She poured Jake's coffee, drank half a cup herself and then told him she would go to bed. It hurt a little that he made no demur, only told her to sleep well, and not to bother to get up in the morning. 'Mrs Turner brings tea when she gets here and she'll get the breakfast. I'll just run through these, there may be something important.'

She stayed awake a long time, too tired to think much about things but too unhappy to sleep, so that when she did at last it was to wake to Mrs Turner's voice.

'Good morning, madam dear. Mr Royle said as how to leave you to have yer sleep out, which I've done, and there's a nice little breakfast waiting for later, so just you drink this and get up when you fancy.'

Annis sat up, very wide awake. 'Mrs Turner— good morning. Heavens, it must be late . . .'

'Nine o'clock just gorn, mum, and Mr Royle been out of the 'ouse this hour or more.'

Annis said hastily: 'Oh, yes of course—he had to be at the office. Did he leave any message?'

Mrs Turner looked surprised. 'No, mum, he'll 'ave told you when 'e'll be 'ome.'

Annis poured her tea and fussed with the milk and sugar. 'Oh, yes, of course—I'm not properly awake.' She smiled at Mrs Turner, who smiled back widely. She had been a little nervous of the house-keeper, but she saw she need not be; Mrs Turner was a younger edition of their own Mrs Wells. She said now: 'Mrs Turner, could you spare the time to show me round this morning, and perhaps there are some jobs I can do to help you? It's a big flat for one and Jake told me that you're a very good cook as well.'

Mrs Turner looked pleased. 'Well, though I says it as shouldn't, I've got a light 'and with pastry. I'll be pleased to take you round, madam, and as for the odd jobs—well, there are always the flowers and such, and bits of shopping . . .'

So the morning passed in a thorough going over of the flat and its contents, and Annis managed to convey in the nicest possible way that she had no intention of encroaching upon Mrs Turner's pre-serves, although they settled between them that she should do the shopping, the flowers and polish the silver if she felt inclined. 'And there's no earthly reason why I shouldn't switch on the washing machine from time to time,' suggested Annis, 'and I do like ironing.'

'Now that would be an 'elp, mum. Mr Royle, as you well know, wears silk shirts and the finest cotton, and the time it takes to get them just so you'd never believe.'

Annis lunched off a tray in the sitting-room while she made a shopping list of the things Mrs Turner would need, then took herself off with her basket. There were shops quite close by, Mrs Turner had assured her, and she had told her how to get to them, elegant shops lining a small street five minutes' walk away, a far cry from the village stores at home, she thought, choosing back bacon with an experienced eye.

Mrs Turner went soon after four o'clock, bringing in the tea tray with her hat on, ready to go. 'And there's a nice steak and kidney pie in the fridge,' she told Annis. 'Just needs a good warm through, the veg are ready to cook, I've done them little peas and baby carrots, and there's a nice sherry trifle—Mr Royle's partial to sherry trifle. I'll say good afternoon, madam.'

'Goodbye, Mrs Turner, and thank you very much. You don't have to get tea for me, you know, I'm sure you've enough to do.'

'Time on me 'ands, mum, with you doing the shopping.'

Annis, pouring her tea, reflected that she was going to have time on her hands too.

Mrs Turner had set the table for dinner, with Spode china and shining silver and glass. There was nothing to do, so she wandered through the flat and presently found a small pile of ironing waiting to be done. She was making an excellent job of the last of Jake's shirts when he came home.

'I'm in the kitchen!' she called as she heard his key in the lock, and looked up and smiled as his head appeared round the door.

He came right in and dropped a casual kiss on her head, then observed in surprise, 'I thought Mrs Turner did the ironing.'

'She did. We've had a nice cosy talk and I said I'd do the ironing and the shopping—it's a big flat to keep clean, you know.'

'Do what you like, Annis. Have you enjoyed your day?'

'Very much. It's all so labour-saving, and the shops are very good . . .' She folded the shirt expertly. 'Not at all like the village stores.'

'Which reminds me, I thought we might go home on Saturday, leave early in the morning and spend an hour there and then go on to your place. We can drive back the same evening and have a quiet Sunday here. Would you like that?'

'Very much—I'll take the presents with me.'

'Your car will be delivered tomorrow. I'll try and get home early and you can try her out.'

Her eyes shone. 'Oh, Jake, thank you!'

'You'll be able to drive down to Millbury when you feel like it.' He went to the door. 'I'm going to have a shower—is dinner at the usual time?'

'Yes, Mrs Turner's put it all ready.'

'Good. By the way, we shall be dining out quite a bit—I've got a number of friends and they want to meet you.'

Annis eyed him uncertainly. 'I'm not awfully good at dinner parties . . . I haven't much conversation.'

He said deliberately: 'I shouldn't worry about that, darling, you're pretty enough to get away without making any effort at anything.'

'Oh, do you think I'm pretty?' She stared at him over the pile of beautifully ironed shirts.

'Why else should I have married you?' he asked carelessly, and went whistling to the bathroom.

On Saturday they left at eight o'clock after breakfast eaten at the kitchen table because Mrs Turner didn't come at the weekends. Annis was surprised when Jake offered to wash up while she tidied the flat. There was a great deal she didn't know about him, she reflected as she collected her bag and a jacket and her shopping basket crammed with presents. She had something for everyone, for Jake's family too. His mother had sounded a little surprised that they weren't staying to lunch, only hoping mildly that they would find time to go to stay for the weekend soon, and as for her own mother, she had been delighted at the idea of seeing them, merely observing that there was always a room for them when they could manage to stay overnight.

But neither mother mentioned the brevity of their visit. They were received warmly at Jake's home, the presents were exclaimed over, Jake's grandmother, brought down to the sitting room to meet them, was unusually quiet, only as they were leaving did she pull Annis down to kiss her. 'A tricky business, marriage, Annis, but you're a good girl. I've no doubt you'll make a success of it.' And she added: 'Only don't take too long about it.'

It was delightful to see her own family again. They came pouring out of the house, Mary and Edward home for the weekend, the three younger ones enveloping her in hugs. The time went too quickly. By the time the presents had been admired, lunch eaten, Nancy inspected and a quick visit to the Averys made, it was time to return to London. And as they began a round of goodbyes, Mrs Fothergill said gently: 'I do hope you'll be able to stay for a night or two soon. I know how busy Jake is—your father has been explaining his work to me. I had no idea that he was quite as important as that.'

It was on the tip of Annis's tongue to say that she had no idea either, but she nodded and smiled and said: 'Oh, yes,' vaguely, and when her mother added: 'You're happy, darling?' she made haste to say that she was—very.

It was her father who declared loudly that they all missed her. 'You really must come for a week or so. Sapphro and Dusty miss you too, not to mention Nancy.'

'And us,' shrilled little Audrey. 'Why don't you come every weekend?'

'Well, we have to go and see Jake's mother and father too,' said Annis reasonably.

Audrey was disposed to argue. 'I don't see . . .' she began with a hint of tears.

Jake swung her high into the air so that she shrieked with delight. 'Tell you what, young Audrey, suppose I bring Annis down and let her stay for a week, would you like that?'

She threw small skinny arms round his neck. 'Oh, Jake, yes, please! But can't you stay too?'

'Me? I have to work.' He gave her a hug. 'But that's a promise.'

They stopped for a meal on their way back to London. Jake hadn't said much as they drove, only as they neared Wootton Bassett he said: 'How about stopping here for dinner? There's a place in the High Street—the Magnolia Room.'

And when they were seated, he looked up from his menu to say 'I enjoyed today, didn't you? You have a delightful family, Annis.'

She smiled at him widely. 'Yes, I know, but your family is nice too—I love your granny.'

'I meant what I said. I'll drive you down and you can stay for a week—better still, you can drive yourself down.'

'I'm a bit scared of the traffic in London.'

'You did well enough the other evening. We'll drive round a bit more if you like—you'll soon get used to it.' He smiled a little and bent his head over the menu again.

Annis studied her own menu, remembering his casual good nature when she had taken her little car round the squares and quiet streets near his flat. He hadn't been impatient at her nervousness, but he had been aloof too; rather like a polite driving instructor. She wondered if he was regretting marrying her—after all, so far she hadn't been much of a companion, as she hadn't had the chance, and she hadn't been a hostess to his friends, either, something she rather dreaded now that they were actually married.

His voice asking her what she would like to eat roused her from her thoughts, and she cast an eye down hastily. 'Oh, the courgettes and mushrooms, I think, and then the sole.' She looked round her. 'This is rather nice, isn't it?'

'Yes, we haven't been out much, have we, Annis?' He smiled at her with such charm that she found herself murmuring that it didn't matter, that he was busy . . .

'I can take it easy for a while. We'll have an evening out soon, and have a few friends to dinner. You'll like that?'

She stared down at the courgettes and mushrooms. 'Oh, yes, I should like to meet your friends.' And that was a fib; she was scared stiff at the very idea.

'They're your friends too,' he observed blandly, and smiled again.

She made coffee when they got in later and they sat drinking it in the sitting room, and she almost dropped her cup when Jake asked abruptly: 'Are you happy, Annis?' and before she could answer: 'Shall we go to the house in Bath and spend a few days? We could visit our families from there . . . I can spare a week.'

'That would be lovely. Oh, Jake, could we really—you wouldn't feel bored?'

He gave her a long considered look. He was on the point of saying something, but he stopped and said lightly: 'Darling, you never bore me.' He got up and poured more coffee for them both and she said quickly:

'Jake, please don't call me darling—I know everyone does but, but—well . . .' She hesitated and he interrupted her silkily:

'You're an old-fashioned girl who thinks that only people who love each other should use the word. Is that it?'

'Yes, Jake. Do you mind?'

'Not in the least, but don't expect me to stop calling my women friends darling, will you? They might think it odd.'

It was impossible to tell if he was angry or amused. Annis waited a minute and when he didn't say any more she asked: 'When shall we go?'

'To Bath? Oh, we might travel down next Sunday. I believe we're to be asked to a party on Saturday, a welcome to the newly married pair.'

'You didn't tell me . . .'

'I thought you might take fright—all my friends will be there.'

She gave him a worried look. 'Whatever shall I wear?'

'I gather it's to be quite an affair—a long dress, I

should imagine. Why not get yourself something?
Pale green, I think, with that hair. I've opened an
account for you at Harrods.'

'You're very kind to me Jake—thank you. I'll find
something.'

He got up as she did. 'Not dark blue velvet,' he
said, and they both laughed. It seemed a long time
ago, another world—a lonely world without Jake,
she reminded herself, and wished him goodnight,
offering a cheek for his light kiss. It would be nice to
give way to impulse and throw her arms round his
neck. While she got ready for bed she speculated as
to what he would do. Nothing, she concluded, but
that was her own fault, she wasn't making any efforts
to attract him. To tell the truth, she was afraid of
being blandly and coolly snubbed. She wished she
had a little more experience of men. Matt was the
only man she had known, and one couldn't count
him.

CHAPTER EIGHT

'It was Jake who wakened her in the morning, sitting on the side of her bed with a tea tray on his knees. Annis shot upright, still only half awake.

'I've overslept . . . whatever is the time?'

'Eight o'clock, and it's Sunday. Church this morning, don't you think? It's pouring with rain, so we can spend the afternoon reading the papers with easy consciences.' He poured tea and when he had had his strolled to the door. 'I never bother with breakfast, but that's because I'm too lazy to cook for myself.'

Annis took the hint. 'Bacon and eggs', she promised, 'in about half an hour.'

It was the kind of day she had dreamed of—just the two of them, with Jake sprawled in his chair and the Sunday papers spread all round them. They had sandwiches and a drink after church and then a long-drawn-out tea with Mrs Turner's fruit cake and a great pile of buttered toast, and in the evening, Annis went into the kitchen and cooked steak and chips and made a salad, then anxious to let Jake know that she could cook, made a rhubarb pie, lavishly topped with clotted cream. And while she was laying the table Jake fetched a bottle of claret: 'Something worthy of that delicious smell coming from the kitchen', he told her.

They had never been so close, Annis thought as

she got into bed and allowed daydreams to take over until she slept.

And as the week passed she began to think that they were getting back to the warm friendship they had had before they married. Perhaps it was being in Lisbon that had made them so uncertain; for Jake had been that, she was sure, perhaps not avoiding her, but certainly not over-eager to be with her, and she herself had felt awkward and stiff. But now that they were back at the flat they were settling into a pleasantly easy way of life together. He came home each evening content, it seemed, to relax over a drink and tell her about his day. Half of it she didn't understand, of course, but she was learning fast. In her turn she told him of her day, glossing over the dull bits, telling him news from her home and his and then after dinner, sitting opposite him working painstakingly over the tapestry work she had bought herself or knitting the complicated sweater Emma wanted for her birthday.

But she didn't tell him about the dress she had bought for the party they were to go to—organza patterned in green, with a pie-frill neck, long tight sleeves and a long full skirt. And since she no longer needed to be so careful over spending, she bought satin slippers to match. They were wildly expensive and no one would see them, but the pleasure she would have in wearing them was worth it.

She was very nervous about the party by the time Saturday came round. She packed for their few days in Bath in the morning and then with Jake drove down to an inn on the Thames outside Maidenhead, where they had lunch, taking their time over it while they made a few plans for their stay in Bath. And since it was a pleasant afternoon and they had time to spare, Jake took a road through Windsor Great Park before joining the A 30 and going back to the flat. They had stopped for tea on the way, so that by the time they got in, it was time to dress.

Annis hadn't told Jake that she was scared of meeting his friends. She dressed in a flurry of nerves and presently joined him in the sitting room with a heightened colour and an outward calm which threatened to turn to hysterics at a moment's notice.

He stood looking at her for a long moment. 'Very beautiful indeed, you'll knock them cold. You'd better have a stiff drink, though, you're wound up like a top.'

'I don't know anyone.' She tried to speak casually and her voice came out in a squeak.

'You know me,' he said, half laughing. 'Come, come, Annis, you've been facing Mothers' Unions and Sunday School and choir practice for years and I think you'll like my friends—I hope they'll be your friends too.'

She swallowed the drink he gave her and followed him meekly out to the car, and just to let him see that she was perfectly at ease, chatted animatedly all the way to Hampstead where the party was being held. And as for Jake, he hardly spoke, only when he stopped the car before an important-looking house in a quiet road, he bent and kissed her cheek. 'I'm very proud of you,' he told her, and got out to open her door.

Contrary to all her worst forebodings, the evening was a great success. They were welcomed at the door and swept into a vast room crowded with people, all smiling and shaking hands and in the case of several elderly gentlemen, kissing her with relish. Just at first she was scared that Jake might leave her, but he stayed by her, an arm through hers. He knew everyone there and there was a good deal of joking and laughter, and after the second glass of champagne, Annis began to relax and enjoy herself. By her own home standards these people were very grand, but they were friendly too and talked about the same things as the people she knew in Millbury—babies and children at school and how difficult it was to get daily help and what did she think of her new home . . .

She was with a small group of people when she found that Jake had gone, and she spent the next few minutes looking for him. Although the room was crowded she was sure he wasn't in it. It was a few minutes later when the music started up and they began to dance that she saw him coming into the room with a slim dark girl in a scarlet dress. She turned her back at once and smilingly accepted a young man's invitation to dance. She didn't like him overmuch, he was extravagantly dressed for one thing, and he stared at her in a way that made her uncomfortable, but any port in a storm.

She wasn't sure what happened next, but there was Jake dancing her off as cool as you please and all she could do was mutter: 'Well, how rude!'

'I suppose it's that red hair that makes you so impetuous,' said Jake softly. 'I could see your dire thoughts from where I was at the door—I thought we'd agreed that jealousy is only for those in love?'

More and more couples were taking to the floor and it was getting crowded. He guided her expertly through the crush and she followed his steps just as expertly. Millbury Village Saturday evening hop had been a splendid breeding ground for all the latest dances. 'I don't know what you mean,' she said airily. 'I just happened to glance in that direction and you . . .' And when he only chuckled, she added: 'She's a very pretty girl. What's her name?'

'I've no idea. She just happened to be in the hall as I was coming out of Howard's study—he wanted my advice about some shares.' He laughed a little. 'This is a splendid party, isn't it?'

'Yes,' said Annis, she knew her voice was peevish, but that was how she felt.

She danced with a great many other men after that and every now and again she found herself with Jake who, while they were dancing together, gave her the impression that he enjoyed it very much and then confused her by handing her over with cheerful willingness to her next partner.

It was towards the end of the evening when they were dancing together again that the music stopped suddenly and their host made his way towards them carrying a silver tray upon which was a small silver coffee pot, a sugar bowl and cream jug. He halted in front of them and everyone closed in to hear what he had to say. He made a neat little speech, handed Jake the tray, wished them both a long and happy married life from all their friends there and kissed Annis heartily. Which was the signal for everyone else to crowd even closer and to shake hands and offer congratulations.

Someone took the tray from Jake and he put an arm round Annis's waist, and when someone cried 'Speech, speech!' he thanked them with a dry humour which had them all laughing.

They drank champagne after that and presently the party broke up. Back in the flat Annis arranged the coffee tray on a sofa table in the sitting room. 'A lovely party,' she observed, and yawned mightily. 'What time do you want to leave in the morning, Jake?'

'No hurry—eleven o'clock will do. Go to bed, Annis, you're tired. I'm glad you like my friends.'

'Oh, I do, I do. Shall we have them all to dinner in turn? I was scared of meeting them, you know, but not any more.'

'We'll certainly have them round, half a dozen at a time.' He was sitting on the arm of a chair swinging an enormous leg. 'You're a remarkably beautiful woman, my dear. I'm very proud of you.'

She had had a little too much champagne, which could have been the reason why she crossed the room and kissed him. 'Thank you, Jake. Goodnight.'

It was raining when they left London the next morning, but by the time they reached Bath the sky had cleared, and a thin sunshine washed over the grey stone of the city, peaceful in its Sunday calm. They had come in from the London Road and Jake turned and twisted down one-way streets until he stopped finally outside the house.

The Bates welcomed them with decorous pleasure and the prospect of one of Mrs Bates' splendid teas, and presently when they had unpacked, gone round the garden and Jake had dealt with the bills tidily laid out for him by Bates, they sat down in the drawing-room and Mrs Bates, who had a poor opinion of anyone else's cooking but her own, trotted in and out with scones and fruit cake, cucumber sandwiches, cut paper-thin, and little chocolate and walnut cakes, all of which she begged them to sample.

'No weight problems, I hope?' asked Jake as Annis poured the tea.

She eyed him with some coldness. 'I'm already on the big side,' she pointed out.

'Ah, yes, but your—er—vital statistics seem to me to be very nicely proportioned.' He wasn't looking at her, so she was able to blush in comfort. 'Mrs Bates will be hurt if we don't try everything at least once.'

So they made a very good tea between them and since Bates had hinted that dinner was to be a very special affair, seeing that it was their first day in their new home, Jake took Annis for a good brisk walk, through the park and past the reference library and across Queen Square into Milsom Street, where they slowed their steps to peer in the shop windows.

To Annis it was heaven. They chose enormous diamond rings, fabulous necklaces and bracelets, shoes with three-inch heels so flimsy that a good brisk walk would have ruined them. There was nothing flimsy about their price, though, as Annis pointed out—they wouldn't be a sensible buy; half a dozen wearings and they would be shabby . . .

Jake turned to look at her. 'Don't you ever buy anything just because you like it and it's pretty?' he asked with a hint of impatience. And then: 'That was a stupid thing to say, wasn't it? I'm sorry.'

'That's all right. I daresay I'll get used to being able to buy what I want when I want it.' She smiled at him. 'I'll need some practice, that's all.'

He grunted, a friendly rumble which could have

meant anything, and stopped before Jolly's shop window. 'Now that's a pretty dress,' he observed, pointing to a gleaming satin gown draped in a tawny chiffon scarf.

Annis pressed her pretty nose up against the window and studied it carefully. 'Yes, it is. But how does one keep the scarf just so for hours on end?'

'Pins, will-power? I wouldn't know. It would go very nicely with your hair. Have you any allowance left?'

She turned to him in astonishment. 'Good gracious, Jake, I've hardly used any of it.'

'In that case we must come shopping tomorrow.'

They walked back briskly through the park, which was a good thing, for Mrs Bates had a magnificent meal for them that evening. 'Their first meal in their new home,' she pointed out, as she supervised Bates' serving with an anxious eye—lobster patties, medallions of beef garnished with a rich cream sauce, with tiny new potatoes and baby green peas, and then a soufflé Harlequin. Annis declared that she had never eaten anything so delicious in her life, and Jake told Bates to open another bottle of champagne and bring Mrs Bates to the dining-room so that they could drink her health. But first Bates requested the honour of drinking the new owners' healths, and made a little speech wishing them happiness and long life, so that dinner took quite a time, and Annis grew heavy eyed over their coffee afterwards. Jake, sitting opposite her, had glanced up from the paper he was reading, and suggested that she should go to bed, and she had gone obediently and was asleep before she thought two coherent thoughts.

She hadn't really believed Jake when he had said

that they would go shopping, which, she had to admit to herself, had been silly of her, as he seldom said anything he didn't mean. They spent the morning in a delightful if expensive fashion and returned for lunch laden with parcels. Not only had he bought her the black dress, but there were elegant satin slippers to match, a quilted silk coat to go over the dress, and an evening bag which, he had decided with careless interest, was just right to go with the slippers. And when she had paused to look into a jeweller's window and admired a rose diamond and pearl brooch, he had bought that too.

She thanked him rather shyly before they sat down to lunch and had her happy excitement considerably doused by his casual: 'Glad you like them—there's no reason why you shouldn't buy these things for yourself, you know. I can afford them.'

Annis made polite conversation over the meal while she pondered that remark—so he'd bought the things because she was his wife and as such had to be suitably dressed, not because he had wanted to give her a present. Disappointment tasted bitter in her mouth; just for a little while she had been hopeful ... She looked up and saw him looking at her thoughtfully, and for lack of anything to say, asked when he wanted to visit his parents.

They went two days later; two days quite nicely filled with shopping for the house, taking long walks and driving out into the country round Bath; it was her mother's birthday in a week or so and Annis had set her heart on finding a silver photograph frame similar to the only one her parent possessed and treasured. Jake had driven her to Stow-on-the-Wold where they had roamed in and out of the antique shops lining the wide old-fashioned street of the pretty little town, and she had found what she was looking for. It had been a good deal more money than she had expected, but Jake, taking one look at her doubtful face, had said: 'That's the one, isn't it? Buy it.' So she had.

She had bought a charming little vase for her mother-in-law too, and a trinket box for Jake's grandmother, and when she had hesitated over some trifle for her father-in-law, Jake had undertaken to get a bottle of whisky for him.

Annis dressed with care for their visit; a Jaegar three-piece of cotton jersey in cream and lime green and the sandals she had bought in Lisbon. She looked incredibly beautiful as she got into the car beside Jake after breakfast, and he told her so; but he uttered the words with the coolness of a polite host wanting to please a guest and she took no pleasure from them. But nothing of her feelings showed; she turned a serene face to him and thanked him nicely.

The day was an unqualified success. Jake's parents greeted her as if she were indeed a daughter and his grandmother, after one or two outspoken remarks about the possibility of a great-grandchild, settled down to cross-examine Annis about her day-to-day activities. Annis obliged willingly enough; there was plenty to tell the old lady, and when she observed again, rather sourly, that she hoped that she wasn't going to be kept waiting too long before she could be a great-grandmother, Annis remarked calmly enough that they hadn't been married very long, had they?

'Long enough,' grumbled their irascible companion, 'but you're a nice healthy young woman, and pretty, too. I hope Jake looks after you properly.'

Annis had said promptly that indeed he did and described the pearl and diamond brooch, aware that Jake was listening to every word and enjoying it.

They spent the whole day there, lunching and then strolling in the garden and presently sitting on the wide verandah at the back of the house. The two men talking in a desultory fashion while Mrs Royle sat beside Annis, gossiping gently about the house in Bath. 'And do you like it better than the London flat?' she had wanted to know.

'Oh, yes, though the flat's pretty super, too, but I've got to get used to it, you see—I've always lived at the Rectory and there's a big garden there and sheds and things, I rather miss that . . .'

They had tea presently and Jake and Annis had gone for a walk afterwards, through the village and up into the wooded hills beyond, and Jake had been a delightful companion, although he hadn't talked about them at all.

Two days later they went to her home, and somehow or other everyone had contrived to be there so that they all talked at once and Annis was dragged here and there to see Nancy, a stray kitten which had been adopted, the bantam chicks which had hatched out, the painting Emma had done of the house . . . there was no end to the things she had to see and admire. She hardly spoke to Jake until they were sitting at lunch, when during a lull in the talk he observed: 'How would you like to come down for a week or two darling? I'm going to be very busy and it might be lonely for you in London.'

She had hesitated, taken by surprise. 'But there are three dinner parties—the Mottrams and the Dawes, and we're having some people at the end of next week, and you suggested we should go to that aunt of yours . . .'

'All dealt with during the next two weeks; after that you'll be free as air.' Jake spoke pleasantly, but she could see that he had no intention of allowing her to argue.

'I'd love to, if Mother will have me.'

The entire family, it seemed, were only too delighted. 'And you'll be able to come down as often as you can, won't you, Jake?' asked Mrs Fothergill comfortably without waiting for him to answer.

On the way home later, Annis asked a question she had made up her mind to ask anyway. 'Why do you want me to come home while you're away? Why couldn't I go with you? You said, before we married, that when you went somewhere I could go too.'

'That was before we married!'

She stared out at the countryside, trying to think of an answer to that, and gave up, but it didn't stop her next question. 'Don't I fit in with your life in London? Don't your friends like me? Don't you want me to be there?'

His voice was cool. 'Are you trying to pick a quarrel, Annis?'

'No, I just want to know, that's all. I—I suppose I feel inadequate.'

'No need—you're being fanciful, that's all. Women don't use their heads.' He gave a little laugh. '"Man with the head and woman with the heart: Man to command and woman to obey; All else confusion". Tennyson—sounds a bit old-fashioned, but he had the right idea.'

'But I'm a person!' began Annis fierily. 'Why should I obey blindly just because you want me to?'

'We're quarrelling again. What shall we do tomorrow?'

And that was the end of that; he'd retreated behind that bland, casual good humour that told her nothing.

But tomorrow was another day. She cheered herself with that thought before she slept that night, and got up the next morning determined to present a pleasant front at all costs. She succeeded very well, exchanging an undemanding talk with Jake, agreeing willingly to his suggestion that they might explore the Roman Baths, and accompanying him with every sign of enjoyment to a concert in the Pump Room in the evening. And she kept it up for the rest of their stay, never once referring to the future and asking no questions at all, although the desire to do so was almost past bearing at times.

They went back to London in the evening and found the flat at its most welcoming, with flowers in the vases, a meal ready in the fridge and a pile of letters for Jake. He picked them up with a muttered excuse and went into his study and shut the door, and Annis, left to herself, unpacked slowly and then got their supper. It was a cold meal and she didn't disturb him, but sat quietly pretending to read until he joined her. She wanted to ask about his mail, if there had been good news or bad, if he was going away, but she merely remarked mildly about the pleasant evening while she wondered what he would do if she threw something at him and demanded to be allowed to share his life.

Over supper he told her briefly that he would be away all day and reminded her that they had two dinner parties that week, and their own the following week. 'Mrs Turner is a tower of strength on these occasions,' he told her carelessly. 'I should leave the arrangements to her.'

Something Annis had no intention of doing. With great difficulty she bit back the hasty remark on the tip of her tongue, and nodded meekly. Her, 'Yes, of course, Jake,' was equally meek, so that he looked at her sharply—a look she met with a charming smile.

The week ran its course and she found plenty to do. She didn't know London well. She formed the habit of going out each day on a voyage of discovery, although she didn't bother Jake with these jaunts when he came home in the evenings. Beyond hoping that she had had a good day, he asked very few questions and so she held her tongue and listened carefully to how his own day had gone. She was a good listener and he seemed to enjoy explaining the intricacies of big business to her. Once or twice, at the end of an evening, when he had relaxed, he would ask her if she wasn't bored with her days, and she answered quite simply that she found plenty to keep her occupied, which was true enough. She had explored the parks, walked miles with a guide book in her hand, watched the changing of the guard at Buckingham Palace and stood, along with a great many other people, outside St Margaret's, Westminster in order to see a society bride emerge after the wedding. She hadn't planned to do it, but she happened to be passing and it seemed too good an opportunity to miss. But all this she kept to herself. Jake wouldn't want to know—indeed, he might laugh at her naïveté.

The dinner parties weren't the frightening affairs she had expected. The first one was given by an older couple with a large family of grown-up and teenage children and they had invited friends of all ages. Dinner was a cheerful noisy affair and Annis, sitting between the two older sons of the family, enjoyed herself hugely. And the second dinner party, although a quite different cup of tea, was just as much fun. The Dawes were young, not long married and extremely sociable as well as very smart. Annis was glad she had worn the black satin dress, for the women guests were all incredibly fashionable. But they were nice to her, too: admiring her dress, envying her hair, wanting to know what she thought of London and being married to Jake. Going home afterwards she discovered that she was no longer nervous about their own dinner party.

That was a roaring success too. She and Mrs Turner had concocted a splendid menu between them and Annis had done some of the cooking; she had arranged the table too—a white damask tablecloth and napkins, the silver polished to an incredible brightness, the very best of the glasses and as a centrepiece, an old-fashioned épergne dripping the flowers she had chosen so carefully from the florists in the next street.

She dressed early in a silvery grey crêpe dress and then donned an apron and went into the kitchen where Mrs Turner was busy at the Aga. Everything was all right, they told each other, smiling like conspirators.

And it was. The chilled watercress soup was delicious, so was the fish; sole grilled simply and served with creamed spinach, and the beef *en croûte* melted in the mouth. Mrs Mottram voiced the opinion that the vegetables tasted as though they had just been picked from the garden, and everyone agreed, and Annis beamed with pleasure like a happy child. And the syllabub to finish this repast and which she had made herself was eaten with such relish that she wished that she had made twice as much of it.

It was when the last guest had gone that Jake, sitting at ease reading the evening paper, observed: 'That was a splendid meal, Annis. Mrs Turner certainly did us proud.'

And when Annis didn't answer he put the paper down and looked enquiringly at her.

She said coldly: 'Don't you credit me with any skills at all? Why should you suppose Mrs Turner did it all?' She gave up being cool and added with a snap: 'I made the soup, and I cooked the vegetables, and I made the syllabub too—and I did the table and baked those little biscuits with the drinks.'

Jake folded his paper and got up. 'My dear girl! I'm sorry if I hurt your feelings—I had no idea that you were so good a housewife. I think you're fantastic.'

She eyed him with mounting rage. 'No, you don't!' she declared in a voice throbbing with temper. 'I can't think why you married me, and I can't think why I married you either!'

She shot off to bed without waiting to hear his answer.

She had it the next morning in an oblique sort of way. Jake had wished her good morning exactly as usual without a word about her show of temper the previous evening and she had done her best to behave just as she always did at breakfast, not saying much, letting him skim through the post, seeing that his coffee cup was replenished. She had been unable to disguise her red-rimmed eyes completely, but she had counted on him not noticing, he so seldom looked at her—really looked. So she was quite taken by surprise when he said, as he gathered up his letters preparatory to going: 'I'll drive you down on Saturday, Annis, I'm sure you'd love a week or two with your family. I'm going to be away a good deal.'

She put down the piece of toast very carefully, just as though it would break otherwise. Her insides had gone very cold. 'Could I not come with you, on some of the trips? I wouldn't get in the way.' She had meant to sound casual, but her voice came out in a gruff mumble.

'Oh, I don't think so. You'll be far happier down at Millbury,' and when she opened her mouth to argue: 'No, Annis, I should like you to go.' He half smiled. 'Remember Tennyson?'

She tried again. 'I'm sorry about last night . . .' She was breaking the toast into tiny pieces on her plate. 'I didn't mean it.'

John ignored that. 'We'll leave directly after breakfast,' he told her blandly. 'Will you telephone your mother and let her know we're coming?'

'Yes.' She tried very hard not to sound eager. 'Will you stay too? Just for the weekend?'

'No—I can't spare the time.'

'Then why did you marry me?' Her voice was a whisper that he didn't hear, because he'd gone.

Then she spent the day packing and making

arrangements with Mrs Turner about the running of the flat, and when Jake came home that evening she did her best to behave as though everything was all right between them; not very successfully, but all the same, she tried.

Everyone was home again by the time they reached the rectory, so that it wasn't noticeable that she and Jake hadn't much to say to each other. They had a leisurely lunch, all talking at once, and after a stroll to visit Nancy and an early tea, Jake declared that he had to go back to London, pleading pressure of work. 'Then you must try to come back next weekend,' declared Mrs Fothergill. 'You work too hard, Jake.' She added: 'And you've been married for such a short time too!'

He had made some laughing reply, said goodbye to everyone and asked Annis to go out to the car with him. Annis strolled down the path with him, conscious that her family were peering from the windows. At the car she asked: 'Will you come next weekend, Jake?'

He gave her a quick mocking look. 'I don't know—perhaps.' He bent and kissed her, his hands on her shoulders. Probably, thought Annis miserably, he knew about the eyes watching too.

'Enjoy yourself, Annis.' He got into the car and drove away with a casual wave as he went. She stood and watched the empty lane, listening to the purr of the engine getting fainter and fainter, so near to tears that instead of going back to the drawing-room she went straight upstairs.

She felt better when she had had a good cry, and when she went downstairs again no one remarked upon her red eyes; it was natural enough for a bride to weep if her husband had to go away, even for a few days.

The week slid away, one placid day succeeding the last. Annis busied herself around the house, although the splendid young woman Jake had found in the village and who came twice a week to do the hard work left her little enough to do. But there was old Mrs Wells to gossip with, Hairy to take for a walk, and little Audrey to amuse when she came out of school, as well as Emma and James home each evening. And when she was at a loose end there was always Nancy to groom and lead into the field at the back of the Rectory now that the weather was warmer.

She had wanted to telephone Jake, write to him, perhaps, but she doubted if he would want it. It was all the more surprising that he should ring her each evening. The calls were brief and totally lacking in any kind of endearment, but they were a comfort to her. The second time he phoned she asked: 'Are you home, Jake?' and was taken aback when he told her carelessly that he was in Copenhagen. And the next evening, he told her without being asked that he was in Oslo. He also told her casually enough, as though it was an afterthought, that he wouldn't be down that weekend.

Saturday and Sunday had never been so long. Annis took Hairy and Audrey for a long walk each day, attended the village whist drive and went to church twice on Sunday, but time dragged. She longed for Monday, so that it would be another week and Jake might come at the weekend.

It was on the Wednesday, when Annis had carried in the lunch and gone to call little Audrey from the

garden, that she couldn't find her. Not particularly
worried, she went into the fields around and called,
then went round the house, but there was no sign of
the small girl. So she went once more into the
garden, in and out of the barns and sheds and
through the wicket gate, then she went indoors, told
her mother briefly that she would go down to the
village and take a look there. 'Audrey often goes to
play with the Banner children, doesn't she? I'll fetch
her back—she's gone and forgotten the time.'

But the Banners hadn't seen her, nor had several
other children Annis encountered. She was on the
point of going back to the Rectory to see if her
small sister had turned up when Mrs Thomas, who
kept the poky little shop which sold everything
from cheap sweets to odds and ends of household
requirements, poked her head round her half open
door.

'If it's your little Audrey who you're wanting, I
seen her not 'alf an hour gone, along with they
tinkers.'

'Tinkers? Which way did they go, Mrs Thomas?'

Mrs Thomas was in the mood for a nice chat.
'Nasty thieving folk, and your little Audrey march-
ing along between two of them—ever so friendly like,
arm-in-arm they were.'

Annis frowned; somehow it didn't sound much like
Audrey, who was on the timid side, especially with
strangers. 'Which way did they go?' she asked.

'Up the 'ill to the downs, love. Got an 'orse and
cart and a couple of sorry-looking dogs.'

She would have gone on for a good deal longer
but Annis, well used to her ways, cut in briskly:
'Thanks very much, Mrs Thomas. I'll pop back

home and tell them to keep lunch hot. I'd better go and fetch her.'

Her mother frowned and looked puzzled when she was told. 'But Audrey never goes off on her own— she knows she mustn't . . .' And her father said thoughtfully 'Tinkers, did you say, my dear? I think perhaps I'd best go after her.'

'I'll go, Father, but will you ring Colonel Avery and make sure she's not there, and if she's not, phone anyone else you can think of who might know where she is—she's only been gone a couple of hours, she can't be far.'

'Probably having a whale of a time and forgotten all about lunch.'

Annis changing into a pair of low heeled shoes as she spoke, said: 'Shan't be long, dears,' and set off through the village, following the road until it turned into a lane and then a rough track winding its way between tall hedges towards the woods at the top.

Annis walked fast. She was a little scared but keeping her head. There was no use in calling Audrey; it was ridiculous to imagine that the tinkers were keeping her small sister against her will, but there was always that remote chance.

She reached the trees at last and took a well worn track to the left, wide enough to take a cart, which would bring her out eventually on the farther side of the trees and on to the wide sweep of downs beyond. She went slowly now, stopping often to listen. But there was no sound, and no smell of wood smoke. It began to rain and she came out on to the high ground clear of the trees, but there was nothing to be seen on the downs beyond; she turned back, retracing her steps, searching each small path as she came to it, until she was back where the track started. There was a similar track on the other side of the wood and she started off once more, making herself go slowly, stopping to listen again. She was half way down the track when she heard the faintest of sounds behind her—footsteps, coming steadily nearer, not hurrying. Her heart thumped with fright, but she made herself turn and face the track behind her. There was a sharp bend a few yards from her, half hidden by undergrowth, and whoever it was wasn't making great efforts to keep silent, although there was no unnecessary noise.

She drew a calming breath and let it out, then gasped as Jake came round the bend. He didn't speak until he reached her. 'Your mother told me where she thought you might be—is there any sign of little Audrey?'

He hadn't greeted her, hadn't even said hullo. Annis swallowed her fright and disappointment and found her voice. 'No, none at all. I've been to the farther edge of the wood and there's no sign.' She added: 'It's getting misty.'

'Every minute,' he agreed cheerfully. 'We'd better keep together and be as quiet as we can. If anyone's here they'll give themselves away sooner or later. I asked your mother to give us an hour. Your father's scouring the other side of the village; the Colonel's with him.' He slid past her and took the lead. 'Is there a hollow anywhere here, where a horse and cart could be sheltered?'

Annis thought. 'Yes, there's a hollow between the tracks and there's a way down, but I don't think I remember exactly where it is.'

'Then we'll look.' He sounded patient and calm

and not in the least worried. 'Probably they've pulled the undergrowth into a screen as they left the track.'

It took them less than ten minutes to find it, searching to and fro in the undergrowth; quite a well worn track, still slippery with last autumn's leaves, edging its way between the trees and going steadily downhill. They were nearly at the bottom when Jake stopped and caught Annis's hand. Just ahead of them a horse whinnied.

A moment later, a few cautious steps further, and they were almost in the clearing. The cart was there, so were the horse and dogs, wet and bedraggled, and three people, a woman and two men, were leaning against the cart, and standing in front of them was little Audrey.

Annis had her mouth open ready to call to her when Jake's hand, cool and firm, closed over it.

Audrey's voice was a shrill indignant treble. 'If you don't let me go, and the dogs and the pony, I'll tell my father of you!' She aimed a childish kick at the nearest tinker's leg and caught him off balance, and while he was hopping around on one leg Jake pounced.

'Here, to Annis!' he called to little Audrey, and as she scuttled away, made short work of the two tinkers. He stood over them rubbing his knuckles and bade the woman just stay where she was while the tinkers pulled themselves together.

But they were in no hurry, sitting on the ground, nursing their jaws, and Jake looked over his shoulder at Audrey, standing, in tears now, with Annis's arm round her. 'What happened, love?' he asked gently. The story came out slowly between sniffs and sobs;

she'd seen the tinkers going through the village while she was leaning over the Rectory gate, and they had been belabouring the pony and kicking the dogs. She had told the tinkers what she thought of them and then, with rather more imagination than truth, told them that her father was a very important man and would see that they were punished. Not unnaturally this disturbed the tinkers, and since by now she was outside the gate, they had walked her off with them, threatening the number of horrible things they would do to the pony and dogs if she so much as squeaked. Later, they promised her, they would let her father know and he could slip them a couple of hundred pounds and she should go free. So she had gone with them, anxious for the animals and a little worried as to whether her father had so much money. 'And I'm hungry,' she finished tearfully.

Annis mopped the small face and hugged her, and Jake said: 'That's my brave girl! We'll go straight home to lunch this very minute—at least, you and Annis go. I'll catch you up.'

His eyes rested on Annis's white face for a long moment. 'I daresay Nancy would like company, and I'm sure we can find homes for the dogs.' He turned away. 'Run along now.'

He had spoken mildly, but Annis knew better than to argue. She waited just long enough to see him pull the men to their feet and put a hand in his pocket for his wallet. He was going to buy the animals, of course; the tinkers, half dead with fright, would be punished enough; they would have to find another pony, for a start.

They were almost home when Jake caught them up, leading the pony and with the two dogs at his heels. It took some time to explain it all to the Rector and his wife, but they were so relieved to see little Audrey again that they accepted the animals without a murmur. So lunch was postponed for yet another half hour while the three beasts were fed and housed and generally tidied up, and by the time they were seated Mrs Fothergill's steak and kidney pie was barely worth the eating. Not that Annis noticed; if she had been served a slice of cardboard she would have eaten it without being aware of it. Jake had come, that was all that mattered. After lunch she would talk to him, ask if they might start again and get back into their former friendly footing.

Only it wasn't as easy as that. Jake went away to talk to her father the moment they got up from the table and he had said that he was driving back to London that evening. Annis washed up in a hurry, fearful of missing him, only to learn, when she at last escaped from the kitchen, that he had left her father in the study not ten minutes earlier and had gone over to see Matt. She set the tea tray ready and wandered out into the garden; she would catch him as he came back. Only he didn't come. She listened to the church clock chiming four, remembering that he had said that he must leave by five o'clock. There would be no time to talk, and she supposed unhappily that he didn't want to. She turned away from the house and her mother's faintly worried gaze and crossed the yard to Nancy's stall. James had just brought her in for the night and was out in the field again, bringing in the pony. The little donkey lifted a lip for the carrot she always got and stood munching it, while Annis leaned against her woolly side.

'I don't know what to do,' said Annis, and flung

an arm round Nancy's neck. 'You see, I can't tell him—at least I do want to, but I'm scared to. He said six months, but it isn't working out, is it? And he bought me all those lovely things. I'll have to tell him some time . . .'

'But not now, I think.' Jake's voice from the door behind her made her grab Nancy's neck so tightly that the little donkey tossed her head. 'I was going to suggest that you might like to come back with me, Annis, but I think it might be better if you stayed another week or two.'

Annis's eyes glinted. 'Don't you frighten me like that again!' she warned him, and then, in a quite different voice: 'But I'd like to go back with you, Jake.' She took her arm from Nancy's neck and stood up, facing him. 'Why don't you want me to come? There must be some reason . . .'

'I think it might be better if we don't see each other for a while.' He looked at her unsmilingly. 'I'm going now, I'll tell your mother that you've decided to stay a little longer.'

Before she had an answer to that, he had gone. Annis very nearly flew after him, but pride forbade that, so she buried her face in Nancy's soft coat and burst into tears instead.

CHAPTER NINE

Nobody said anything when she went back into the house. Her father had gone to his study, Emma and James were already busy with their homework and little Audrey was in the kitchen, brushing the dogs. She had quite recovered from her adventure with the tinkers, largely because Jake had made light of the whole episode. When Annis went into the kitchen, Audrey looked up from her task with the information that Jake had given her ever such a lot of money so that she could buy food for the dogs and hay for the pony and have the vet as well. 'He says Hairy and Sapphro won't mind having them here a bit, he says animals understand such things, he says I'm a brave girl, he's going to send me the biggest box of chocolates he can find!' Little Audrey paused for breath. 'I like Jake, I wish he didn't always go away again as soon as he gets here.'

'So do I', agreed Annis so fervently that her small sister took a good look at her.

'You've been crying,' she pronounced. 'You never cry—is it because Jake's gone away?'

Annis bent to stroke one of the dogs; he was elderly and uncertain of his luck still, but after a few moments stroking he closed his eyes and grinned as she tickled his ears. 'Yes,' she said at last, 'I miss him very much, darling.'

'Well, you've got him for ever, anyway, haven't you?' observed Audrey, 'and you can always go after him—think how nice it would be for him to go home and find you there.'

'Yes, I'd thought of that too, but you see he won't be there—he has to travel quite a bit to other countries.'

'Well, next time he'll have to take you with him. He was super today, wasn't he? I didn't mind a bit once I saw him though did you? He looked so furious, didn't he?' Audrey sighed happily. 'What an adventure!'

'Yes, love, but I don't think we want another like that—we were all a bit worried about you, you know.'

'Me? I thought it was you—I heard Mummy tell Daddy that she was ever so worried about you . . .'

'Oh, well, I daresay you didn't hear properly—it was you frightening the lives out of us.' Annis stood up. 'Shall we take Hairy for a walk and leave these two to have a snooze? We'll feed them again when we come in and take them out after tea in the field and let them meet Hairy there, they're more likely to be friends that way.'

The rest of the day seemed endless, and Sunday was even worse, although she filled it from end to end with walking the dogs, going to church, cooking Sunday dinner, grooming Nancy and the dogs, and the pony and helping James with his Maths. And even with all this activity, she didn't sleep a wink, and got up heavy-eyed and utterly miserable.

The moment breakfast had been cleared away she went into the study and picked up the phone. She was past caring what Jake thought. She would have to tell him that she loved him even if it meant never seeing him again, because that was what it would be, she had decided during the long night. He only wanted a pleasant companionship, someone to come home to and entertain his guests. What a fool she had been to have imagined anything else! She dialled the flat and got no reply, but she hadn't really expected it, so she dialled Jake's office. Miss Butt, his personal assistant, answered; an efficient lady, who appeared to work all hours effortlessly and without ever getting in the least bit flustered or untidy. No, she said briskly, Mr Royle was away from the office, she wasn't sure when he would be back, would Mrs Royle like to leave a message in case he phoned in later on?

'No,' said Annis, 'thank you, Miss Butt. Where is my husband?'

'Naples, Mrs Royle.' There was a faint note of surprise in Miss Butt's voice because Annis didn't know that.

Annis didn't hesitate. 'Will you book me on a flight there first thing tomorrow morning, please? I'm driving up today and I'll call in the office and pick up the ticket.'

Miss Butt's efficiency was slightly dented by surprise. 'Mr Royle may have already left . . .'

'I'll chance that. Will you let me know where he's staying—and thanks.'

She rang off before Miss Butt could spoil her plans with sensible suggestions.

Her mother was surprisingly matter-or-fact about it when Annis went to tell her. 'What a nice idea,' she observed. 'I'm sure Jake will be thrilled to see you.' She didn't seem to notice Annis's silence. 'How will you go, dear?'

'If Father could drive me into Yeovil I'll get the afternoon train, that will give me time to pack a few things and collect my ticket from Jake's office.'

'Yes, dear. Why bother to take everything with you? You can fetch the rest of your things when you come next time—so much easier with the car.'

If there'll be a next time, thought Annis dolefully, and the next moment told herself not to be so faint-hearted.

The flat, thanks to the redoubtable Mrs Turner, looked welcoming, and now that she had added a few bits and pieces around the place, almost like home. She left a note for Mrs Turner who would be back to sleep later, and took a taxi to Jake's office, on the third floor of a palatial building in the City, where she found Miss Butt sitting neatly behind the desk in her office, using a typewriter as though it were a grand piano.

She lifted her hands gracefully as she saw Annis and laid them in her lap, for all the world like a concert pianist, and Annis, a trifle lightheaded by now, suppressed a giggle.

'Good afternoon, Mrs Royle. I have your ticket—your flight is at nine o'clock from Heathrow, you should be in Naples in time for a late lunch. I've also obtained some money, both English and Italian, from the bank—I wasn't sure you would have the time . . .'

Annis could have hugged her. She had forgotten about money; she had some with her, of course, but possibly not enough. 'Oh, how very thoughtful of you, Miss Butt,' she said thankfully. 'I'd forgotten that.'

Miss Butt gave her a kindly smile and said in a

superior voice: 'Mr Royle relies upon me to remember these things, Mrs Royle.'

'Oh, I'm sure he does, he thinks the world of you,' said Annis. She took the ticket and the money and started for the door, accompanied by Miss Butt.

'If I may say so, Mrs Royle, you don't look too well. I hope you won't find the flight too much for you.'

It wasn't the flight Annis was dreading, but what would happen when she got to Naples and Jake discovered that she had followed him. 'I expect I'll be O.K.' Even in her own ears her voice sounded very uncertain.

Money did make a difference, thought Annis, sitting in comfort in the plane, watching England grow smaller beneath her. It solved so many small problems—a taxi to the airport, never mind the fare, porters and coffee, an armful of magazines to keep her from thinking too much about meeting Jake—if he was there. That was something she would have to face, but not until it became necessary. She drank the coffee which was offered her and opened one of the magazines, to stare at one page and go on thinking. Her family had been sweet. Her mother had undertaken to let Jakes' mother know that they were both abroad. She would let Matt know too—Annis remembered that she had said that she would go over to the Manor that afternoon and go for a walk with him. Little Audrey hadn't said much, only hugged her and begged her to come back soon and bring Jake with her, and she was to be sure and tell him that the pony and the dogs were settling in very nicely and could he help her to think of names for them.

Annis shut the magazine and leaned back and closed her eyes; she hadn't slept much during the night, but now she had, so to speak, reached the point of no return and there was nothing else to do. For no reason at all she remembered what Jake had said: 'Man with the head and woman with the heart . . .' Perhaps that was where the trouble lay, he cool and detached and deliberate, and she rushing into something just because her heart told her to. He had been so calm, almost casual, when they had found little Audrey, if he had had any feeling for her at all surely he would have acted differently . . . She drifted off into sleep and didn't wake until the air hostess asked her to fasten her seat-belt.

She reached the hotel soon after two o'clock, paid the taxi driver and went inside. Mr Royle was indeed staying there, the clerk at the desk told her, but was out at the moment. Would madam care to wait?

The clerk looked at her admiringly. She stood, her hair glowing above her pale face and her eyes enormous from too little sleep. A light meal, he suggested or a cool drink and perhaps a tray of tea in half an hour or so? The foyer was very comfortable and madam could rest. And her luggage?

Annis pointed to the Gucci overnight bag which was all she had brought with her. 'If I could just wait here?' She smiled at the clerk, who came round from behind the desk and led her to a cushioned cane chair, put her case down beside her and snapped his fingers at a passing waiter.

The long cool drink revived her and presently she found her way to a palatial powder room, where, surrounded by marble and blue velvet, she re-did her face and her hair. She was very pale, the result of fright at what she was doing, the flight and quite forgetting to have any lunch, otherwise she didn't look too bad. Her knitted cotton three-piece was the height of fashion and suited her, her sandals and handbag were exactly right: she studied herself in the long mirror very carefully, anxious to give a good impression—cool, poised and assured—when Jake saw her.

She went back to her chair and sat down, doing nothing, not noticing the people coming and going all around her, her eyes on the door. And an hour went and another half hour. Not long now, she promised herself, and because she was tired and lightheaded from hunger, closed her eyes.

When she opened them, Jake was sitting in the chair opposite her. She wasn't cool or poised or assured, she looked like a small girl who had been naughty and expected to be punished.

'Hullo,' said Jake gently. 'Shall we have tea? You look as though you could do with it.'

'I didn't mean to go to sleep.' Annis put a hand up to her hair and he said:

'No, leave it, it looks nice.' He beckoned to a hovering waiter and ordered tea, then he sat back in his chair. 'Is there something wrong at home?' he asked, still gently.

Annis shook her head. She was on the verge of tears: everything had gone wrong; what in heaven's name had possessed her to go to sleep, probably she had been snoring too. She pleated the skirt of her dress with hands that shook and didn't look at him. She was still searching desperately for something to say when the tea arrived and Jake poured her a cup and put it into her hands.

'Lunch?,' he queried, and held out a plate of tiny sandwiches.

She sipped her tea and found her voice. 'I forgot.' She drew a deep breath. 'Jake, I must talk to you . . .' She broke off and looked around her. The foyer had filled up with little groups of people, the women very smart, the men prosperous looking. 'Not here,' she added urgently.

He put down his cup and crossed his legs, the picture of a man who was comfortable and didn't want to move. 'I hardly think you would have come all this way for a little teatime chat,' he remarked mildly, 'but do have some more tea—we'll go for a run in the car presently. I'll go and have a shower and be with you in ten minutes or so.'

He picked up his dispatch case and added casually: 'I'm booked on the seven o'clock flight home, by the way.'

Annis gazed up at him in utter panic. Her head was filled with terror strongly mixed with rage, there was only one urgent thought in her mind: to get away fast. While he was having his shower, she'd go . . . she had no idea, but she'd go.

Jake was watching her telltale face. 'I shouldn't if I were you,' he advised her softly. 'You can't run away for ever, Annis, and it's a long way to have come, just to chicken out at the last moment.'

The rage was uppermost. 'Chicken out? What a simply beastly thing to say, and what do you know about it anyway?' Her pale face was flushed now and her eyes flashed.

'Perhaps more than you think,' he told her, and walked away, not hurrying.

She fumed for thirty seconds or so, aware that he

was quite right; of course, it would be silly to go back tamely without having said what she intended to say and got it over with. She went back to the blue velvet and marble and did her face and hair once more, then went back to sit, very dignified, until Jake reappeared.

He looked pleased with himself, which was annoying. He also looked very tired, which made her loving heart ache with sympathy, so that she got to her feet meekly enough and went out to where a Porsche Carrera was waiting.

In answer to her enquiring look Jake said: 'Rented—I have to get around, and it's time-saving.' He opened the door for her and then went round to the driving seat, switched on and joined the tangle of traffic going out of the city.

After a minute or two Annis asked: 'Are we going to the airport? How will I get back?'

He glanced at his watch. 'There's plenty of time for that. We're going to Pompeii; it'll be nice and empty of tourists by now, and you can improve your mind while you're saying your piece.'

She had always wanted to see Pompeii, but not in such circumstances. Besides, she had to concentrate on what she wanted to say, and it would be impossible there. 'There's no need,' she began. 'Couldn't we just stop for a few minutes?'

'Impossible, my dear girl. Just look at the traffic— no one stops. It would be almost impossible to get going again.' They paused briefly to pay the toll as they joined the motorway. 'Tell me,' he said blandly, 'what are your plans?'

Annis hesitated. She really hadn't made any: she hadn't looked farther than seeing him and talking to

him. 'I haven't any,' she told him baldly. 'At least, I
hadn't, but I'll get a room at the hotel if you
wouldn't mind taking me back before you drive to
the airport.

'You plan to stay in Naples?' his voice was silky.
'Did you leave your luggage at the airport?'

Her face was very pale again. Her anger had left
her; she felt miserable and hopeless and wondered
for the hundredth time what had possessed her to
embark on such a harebrained scheme. Jake couldn't
care less if she loved him; he would be charmingly
polite and unfeeling and briskly businesslike. 'Man
with the head,' she muttered, not knowing that she
had said it out loud, and Jake, who had heard her,
didn't choose to say so.

'I haven't any luggage,' she said into the silence
between them, 'just my night case.'

And since Jake had nothing to say to this, she
looked out of the window at the mountains looming
a mile or two away.

'Vesuvius is the one on the right,' said Jake, and
she stared at it without speaking. It wasn't a bit as
she had imagined it to be, but then neither was
Naples—the little bit of it that she had seen.
Someone had said: 'See Naples and die.' She felt
like that too, but not for the same reasons.

Pompeii was some thirteen miles from Naples and
they were there in ten minutes. Jake parked the car
under the trees opposite the entrance and they went
through the gate where he bought their tickets, and
up the sloping path, over the cobbled road and under
the low archway into the city. There were few people
about, mostly couples and solitary students with
guide books, and a happily noisy family with a great

many children on their way out. They called out as
Jake went past and he answered them with a laugh.
He sounded positively happy, thought Annis crossly,
and stood obediently while he explained that the
stones under their feet were two thousand years old,
that the dust between them was volcanic dust, just
as old, and did she know that there were some
splendid Doric pillars in the Forum?

She wasn't quite sure what a Doric pillar was,
and at that moment she really didn't care. She
mumbled a reply and tried to recall the words of her
carefully rehearsed speech, only to find that she
couldn't. There was only one thought in her head;
that she loved Jake and never wanted to leave him
again, and that it was quite pointless because in a
very short time now he would be gone—back to
England. Of course she could go with him if she
asked, but pride forbade that—besides, by the time
she had said her piece, she would be too embarrassed
to stay with him. Her mind boggled at the thought
of getting herself home. She had been a fool to come
in the first place, but now she was here, she'd jolly
well do what she had come to do. She would also
make it quite clear that Jake didn't have to do anything about it.

They had reached the Forum by now and she
stood still again while he pointed out with tiresome
exactitude the courthouse, the magnificent arches,
the still standing walls of two-thousand-year-old
bricks, and when she had turned her head this way
and that he had twice twirled her round and pointed
ahead of her. 'And that's Vesuvius . . .' Seen like
that, through the ruins, it looked decidedly more
menacing and rather grand.

There was no one near them, now was the moment
... but Jake caught her arm and said: 'There's
something you have to see, the house of the Vetii—
it's a perfect example of a well-to-do merchant's
house, and the friezes are wonderful.'

He hurried her along narrow streets lined with
the shells of houses and finally into one of them, and
just for a brief spell Annis forgot her own worries.
It could have been any house, allowed to fall into
disrepair. Most of the rooms were without damage,
their walls were painted with colours chosen by
some housewife all those years ago, there were
murals on the dining-room wall, painted by some
long-dead artist, an almost perfect frieze in another
room, a charming little garden on to which the
rooms opened, a miniature centre courtyard. Annis
ran a careful finger over the stone carving of a small
boy's head. 'Oh, I wish Father could see this,' she
said.

'We'll certainly arrange that', commented Jake.
'Your mother, too.'

And when Annis stared at him, on the point of
explaining at last why that wouldn't be possible, he
took her arm and led her out of the house back into
the sunlit street again.

'That house belongs to the dead,' he said firmly.
'Our problems have nothing to do with them.'

He took her hand and led her back the way they
had come, back to the Forum. It was quite empty
now, the tourists had long since gone, even the students and the couples had left in search of coffee or
drinks in one of the cafés outside the gates. It was
now or never. Annis came to a halt by the temple of
Jove, staring at the magnificent ruin with unseeing

eyes, determined to stay that way and not look at Jake.

'I'll be quick,' she began, 'because it must be almost time for you to go—you have to be there an hour before the plane leaves . . .' She broke off and started again. 'I expect you think I'm quite mad coming here like this, but you see I didn't know you were here—I mean, I had to ask Miss Butt. I couldn't wait until you came home. Anyway, I wasn't sure if you wanted to see me again . . .'

'Go on', prompted Jake in a voice which gave nothing away.

'Jake, it's not going to work, is it? Us being married. You've been so kind and generous and patient, but it's quite hopeless. I'm not—that is, I don't think I'm right for you—you keep sending me home . . .' She choked on a sob, but she had the bit between her teeth now and wasn't going to give up. 'I said some horrid things to you and I'm sorry; I didn't mean them, you know, but I was frightened. I thought everything would be all right again the other day when little Audrey disappeared, but all you did was tell me to stay at home—and you didn't look a bit upset . . .'

Jake said very gravely: 'If I'd wasted time being upset, the tinkers would have had the advantage.' He was standing behind her and now he flung a casual arm over her shoulder. 'But go on, Annis.'

'Well, that's all really. There is just one more thing—why I came. I thought I'd better tell you before you . . . that is, before we saw each other again. You did say, before we married, that perhaps we'd get to like each other, even have an affection . . .' She was beginning to gabble, anxious to get it over with. 'Well, I've fallen in love with you, Jake, and I can't go on living with you, just pretending to be a good comrade. I've thought about it a lot and I don't think it would work.'

'I'm damned sure it wouldn't work.' Jake swung her round and put the other arm round her too. 'Tell me, who were you talking to in the barn?'

She said stupidly: 'What barn? Oh, the barn at home. I was talking to Nancy, if you must know. I had to tell someone.'

'Then why didn't you tell me?' he asked softly.

'I did try, only you were always going somewhere: I thought you were avoiding me.'

'Well, I was, my darling.' And when she made an indignant effort to get free: 'No, love, stay where you are, that's where you belong—and listen to me. I fell in love with you the moment I set eyes on you, but I didn't know it at once, and you didn't think much of me, did you? I had to play it very cool, and once we were married it seemed logical to give you time to learn to love me too. And once or twice I thought I'd failed.'

He lifted her chin with one hand and she looked up and saw the love in his face. 'Then you don't mind my coming all this way? Just to tell you?'

Jake bent his head and kissed her slowly. 'My dearest darling, it's the most wonderful thing in the world that you came.'

Annis kissed him back; it was very satisfying, to say the least. 'Yes, but you're going back this evening. Can I come with you?'

'No, because we're not going. I phoned from the hotel before we left and cancelled my flight. I phoned Miss Butt too, she can cope for another few days. Our honeymoon is long overdue, my darling, and this is a very good place in which to have one.'

Annis leaned back in his arms to look at him. 'There are several things,' she began, 'to talk about . . .'

'Not now, dear heart. I can't help thinking that talking for the moment would be a great waste of time.'

He was holding her so tightly that she could hardly breathe, but there was really no need for her to say anything, and in any case, she agreed wholeheartedly.

Harlequin® Plus

A WORD ABOUT THE AUTHOR

Betty Neels, whose first Harlequin was published in 1970, is well known for her stories set in the Netherlands. This is not surprising. Betty is married to a Dutchman, and she spent the first twelve years of her marriage in Holland. Today she and her husband, Johannes, return there as often as three times a year.

As Betty travels, always visiting some fresh spot in Holland, she chooses houses, streets and villages to use in her books; whenever possible she will venture inside privately owned buildings. "And of course," she laughs, "I tend to go through life eavesdropping on conversations in buses and trains and shops." An excellent way, we think, to garner ideas for romance novels.

Betty Neels is a retired nurse. Today she and Johannes make their home in a small three-hundred-year-old stone cottage in England's West Country, where, she says, life moves along at a pleasantly unhurried pace.

Harlequin Romances

The books that let you escape
into the wonderful world of romance!
Trips to exotic places… interesting
plots… meeting memorable people…
the excitement of love…. These are
integral parts of Harlequin Romances –
the heartwarming novels read by
women everywhere.

Many early issues are now available.
Choose from this great selection!

Choose from this list of Harlequin Romance editions.*

Some of these book were originally published under different titles.